CW00722825

The Mrs. Club

Ekene Onu

Copyright 2007 by Ekene Onu

All Rights Reserved

ISBN: 978-0-6151-8077-9

This is a work of fiction. Names, characters, places and incidents either are the product of the author's imagination or are used fictitiously, and any resemblance to any actual persons, living or dead, events or locales is entirely coincidental.

Titi

Champagne taste, Beer pocket!

As I walked into the ballroom, I paused to smooth out a slight crease in my gown. All eyes were on me and why not? I was looking every bit the diva in my red couture gown. The satin fabric highlighted my curves and the deep neckline made me look even more endowed than I already am. Move over ladies, Titi is in the building!

I had chosen my outfit and coordinated my whole look so carefully that you would have thought I was going to the Oscars as a nominee. I had even had my make-up professionally done and put a custom blended weave in my hair. I was so on point; I mean I was totally Tyra meets Gabrielle Union and I was loving it. Top it off with a few carefully chosen pieces of jewelry and there I was -- looking like a million bucks.

You might be wondering why I had gone through all of this effort. Truth be told, on any given day, I'd be considered an attractive woman. Okay, I'll stop being modest, I am hot! I have this whole sexy vibe going but tonight was special: it was the annual Nouveau Africana gala evening. It was being held at the Ritz Carlton in Buckhead and the event brought out the crème de la crème of Africans in America.

So you see, to me this event was even more important than walking the red carpet. The place would be teeming with rich eligible African men and my plan tonight was the same as it had been for the past year…to find a husband.

Yes, I said it; I believe in being open, after all you never know who has a single investment banker friend looking to settle down. What's more, I am not afraid to admit that these days I have to work a little harder and be more strategic because…well, I am on the wrong side of 30.

You see in the African community, age is definitely not on a woman's side. When you are about 22, you are put in the front window and are marked for sale. Then when you are about 26, they mark you 50% off, 75% off when you are 28 and then when you are 30, the sign is changed to say: "ALL GOODS MUST GO!"

Now before you brand me as desperate, you should know that I have had many marriage proposals. After all a babe like me has a lot to offer: beauty, brains, and the ability to fully break it down in the bedroom on a regular basis! What? Why are you looking so aghast?! What is wrong with a woman enjoying sex and not being ashamed to say so?

My problem is I haven't quite found proper husband material and, for me, husband material means not just good looks, but also money and prestige. And when I say money I mean a lot of it. That's right, I'm not saying I'm a gold digger; but hey, a woman has to keep up or at least improve her lifestyle! Look, I don't believe in faking the funk. I am a straight-up person and there is no shame in my game; so yes, I am looking for a husband but he better be rich, African and fabulous!

Every year Nouveau Africana Inc. hosts a benefit for AIDS treatment in Africa and it has become the signature event of the African social season, a veritable who's who. Let me tell you, everyone was there, from Emeka Anayo, the NBA rookie of the year, to Dr. Agu, the first African immigrant to be named on the Forbes 100 list. If I told you the hoops I had jumped through to get tickets, you wouldn't believe me; but suffice it to say, it's not easy trying to be among!

But it looked like all my hard work would pay off. The evening had just started and I had already spotted three well-known millionaires. They were not contenders because they were all married and right now, I have no interest in married men, even though they quite frequently have an interest in me. Well, let me be honest, I might allow them to buy me the occasional Vuitton or trinket, but as far as starting an affair, forget it. I am much too focused on being a wife, so I can't be investing in bad karma.

Fortunately there were some interesting bachelors there also. I spotted Dele Thompson, CEO of Thompson Engineering; he was actually featured in *Fortune* magazine and his net worth was estimated at close to $15 million. Add that to the fact that he is handsome, under 40 and from one of the big name families in Nigeria and you have a lethal combination. I was glad he was noticing me in my sexy red dress noticing him. Naturally his date noticed me as well and gave me the dirtiest of looks as she held on to his arm for dear life. I didn't take it personally, after all 'e no dey hard make person ting become person ting abi'. Let me translate: one person's thing can easily be taken by another. I wasn't feeling like any drama that night so I moved on. But I fully intended to check out Dele when the time was right, girlfriend or not!

Sitting in the corner I saw Dan Okoli, or Dr. Dan as they call him. He had just been featured in *Atlanta* magazine for pioneering some new surgery technique. He certainly meets my criteria in the finance department but as far as looks go, well let's just say that he is not quite my style. I mean this guy is barely 5' 8", is chubby and suffers from a case of adult acne. So even though Danny boy is seriously hot for me, I keep him on the back burner with the heat turned down real low. He waved when he saw me and tried to come over. I quickly looked away and walked in the opposite direction. Can't settle for small fry now, not when the fishing is still good!

And there was JJ Brisbee, my kind of guy: tall, handsome, sexy and very, very rich. His family has had money for generations and he is the official heir. On top of that, JJ has made his own fortune in American media. Word is he is even producing Hollywood movies. Like I said, JJ completely meets my specifications; in fact, just seeing him does the kind of things to me that no polite woman should admit to in public.

Unfortunately JJ is a 'love them and leave them' kind of guy. We had had our fling and it was too much! I mean the guy had me turned out. We would be partying in London one night and Ibiza the next. In the bedroom, the man took it to another level. The problem though was that he wouldn't stop there, he kept taking it to the next level and the next. Forget ménage à trois, JJ is about full-blown orgies. One day he took me to a swingers' club and my darlings, that's when I ran for dear life. I may be bad, but this one is more than Michael Jackson!

Anyway he was there with one virginal looking girl. I heard they are engaged and that the chick is very conservative. You see men? They want to marry angels and have someone shagalicious on the side. The foolish boy winked at me as we made eye contact. Idiot, he gave some other babe a four carat rock, but he still wants to rock my own yansh! Utter nonsense! I gave him an evil look and moved the heck on.

Look at me going on and on about the guys at the gala. Naturally there were also many babes. In fact, let me gist you. As you get to know me you will know there are two things I am very good at: selling homes and getting gist!

So when I entered the place, the first thing I saw was another red dress, but the babe wearing it was nowhere near as correct as me. The babe was at least 40 pounds overweight and the dress showed more than a few curves, if you know what I mean. Plus her blond weave was a little overdue for a touch up. My babes, let me tell you one thing, if you have the audacity to get a blond weave, I am begging you, please invest in a professional touch up at least every now and then. This babe was looking like a complete disgrace, then she turned around and what did I see -- she was none other than Tigi Simpson.

Tigi Simpson! This was a babe that used to be super hot about ten years ago, I mean she was my hero! At the time she could have had her pick of eligible men, but as the story goes, she was busy looking for Mr. Totally Perfect and now look at her. She is still single and looking run down, settling to be the consort of whoever would have her for the night. Judging from the fact that her dress was a Donna Karan from four seasons ago, either the level of men or their frequency had diminished.

"Titi! my darling," she called out to me. I cringed as she walked over; I didn't want to be associated with this aging senior babe. I mean I am still fresh and hot and definitely not broken down. "Hi Tigi," I said unenthusiastically.

"So we are the babes in red; I trust you to be as hot as me now. I see I taught you well," she cooed at me, linking her arm through mine as she steered me towards the bar. This woman was indeed crazy. Was she comparing herself to me? That was like comparing a '94 Honda, to a 2006 C-class. The babe needs to get a grip. Imagine saying that I was as hot as her; doesn't she know sexiness is like microwave oatmeal, leave it in for too long and it will turn dry, sticky and lumpy.

But I didn't want to kick a girl when she was down so I said nothing. Nothing about the fact that I am a good ten years younger and the fact that I will get married and probably be a mother of the cutest little baby by the time I'm her age. Nothing about the fact that her time has come and passed and, guess what, she missed it. Nothing about the fact that instead of trying to get me to buy her a glass of hpnotiq, she needed to be home figuring out her life plan.

Yes O, I'm a nice girl, so I didn't say anything. I just pulled out my purse to pay for the drinks, hpnotiq for her and a whiskey sour for me.

Now, just as I put my Prada clutch on the counter, who placed their hand over mine and said, "let me," but JJ himself.

"It's not everyday a man has the honor of being with two sexy ladies in red," he said, grinning, not even trying to hide the lust in his eyes.

"JJ darling, how are you? I hear you are off the market now," Tigi said, leaning into a hug and a cheek kiss. If you ask me her hips were a little too close to his and his hand was way down her back, practically on her butt and if I was not mistaken he gave it a little squeeze. Na wa for guys, I beg where is his wife to be, she better come get her man.

"Not yet Tigi, and if you two ladies would do me the honors, I could show you just how available I really am." He actually licked his lips as he said it.

The horror of it all! I took off immediately. Tigi could flirt with him if she wanted to; but, like I said, me -- I had plans of being a Mrs. so I couldn't fool around and be known as a shameless ho.

I walked away from the bar and ran smack dab into my girls, Mina and Amaka! We all went to college together and had formed a tight friendship ever since. We are all so different, but there's nothing like spending some years at an all-white college in the middle of upstate New York with nothing else to do on the weekends than tip cows to bond people together. We had been through so many experiences together, from culture shock to racism.

I remember that first winter at Johnston U. It snowed and while the snow was beautiful and new to us African babes, we were completely unprepared for it. That night we were going to a meeting in a nearby dorm and we had, of course, dressed up as usual. Colorful sweaters (it was a decade ago, ok almost two!) matching accessories and cute shoes. When we started to leave our dorm, people kept looking at us strangely. I looked at Mina in her pink sweater with pink hoops and black leggings with patent leather loafers and she looked fine. Maksy looked cute in an oversize orange sweater and black jeans with her new lace-up shoes that she bought from Wild Pair. And as for me well, let's just say I looked fly; so I couldn't understand all the looks we were getting.

Finally someone asked us as we approached the door if we didn't know it had snowed, and weren't we going to wear boots? We all laughed at the suggestion that we would ever wear those ugly construction worker boots that every one seemed to have. Please, you know how true Naija babes are, be fine or die!

My friends, let me tell you there is no teacher like experience! After the three of us slipped and slid our way to the dorm no one told us when we went to buy the boots. We learned that when it came to the weather, function must always come before fashion. That was one of the many experiences that bonded us together. We are all so different but these girls are my sisters.

"Can you believe Yinka would date a guy like that?" Mina said to me, interrupting my trip down memory lane. She was looking at Yinka Davies, an acquaintance of ours.

"A guy like what?" I asked.

"As if you don't know; my goodness, he used to be the security guard in her building." Mina looked disdainfully at the couple who were holding hands while making the rounds.

"I thought he owned a security company?" Amaka said.

"Well, he does now; but it's nothing big. Clearly she is going to be the breadwinner in that relationship," Mina said turning away from the couple who had started dancing now.

"They look so happy though," Amaka said.

"I know," I agreed, watching them. Yinka had her head on his shoulder and he had both his hands around her waist.

"Whatever!" Mina interrupted. "Let's see how happy she is when she realizes he is not in her class."

Mina is such a snob. She's my friend so I can say it. She has a wonderful heart but she can be so pretentious. She married a fairly wealthy guy, I mean they are not JJ-rich; but you know, he is a cardiothoracic surgeon, so he does alright. Meanwhile she stays home and plays the role of a lady who lunches. As far as I can see her main palaver right now is the fact that she hasn't had a child in four years of marriage, and her in-laws are beginning to stress. Other than that, honestly her own is better. I mean her husband is probably the sweetest, most down-to-earth guy I have ever known. Actually, how they got together remains a mystery to me, but c'est la vie. I mean I am not totally knocking her, she is my friend and all but I have to call a cutlass a cutlass, the babe has issues.

She was standing to the side looking down her nose at everyone. Looking every bit the ice princess in her pewter Vera Wang gown, with her hair pulled back into a rather severe chignon. She looked very elegant though, but I guess it's easy to look elegant when you are a size 2, café au lait complexioned and have naturally wavy auburn hair.

"By the way, Titi, what were you doing with that crass woman?" she asked, still speaking in the pseudo British accent popular with the stuck-up Naija set, crinkling her nose in disapproval.

"Who, Tigi? You know she's not that bad." I suddenly felt the urge to defend the poor girl.

"Well whatever, I wouldn't be caught dead talking to her," Mini said, turning up her nose even further.

"Ah ah, Mina, that's rather harsh; cool down I beg jo," I replied a bit impatiently. Even though we were friends, Mina always managed to cause an argument when we were together.

Amaka, our other friend, defended me by saying, "Mina, how far now; the woman is not stressing you so forget about her, please."

Mina glared at her and Amaka ignored her, turning to me. "Anyway, Titi my dear, you are looking hot in that dress." That was Amaka, always the peacemaker, the woman fit be a diplomat.

"My dear, I dey try, and you are looking pretty hot yourself."

She really was actually. Amaka was forever obsessing about her weight, but she was one of those few women that the extra pounds actually looked good on. She was about a size 14, with the kind of velvet chocolate complexion people longed for, and she was wearing the hell out of a bronze gown that she said was a Richard Metzger. Well, that's a designer who definitely knows his way around a curve. I know he does plus sizes but I wonder if he can do anything with a busty size six?

"Thanks," Amaka said, breaking into my reverie, "50% off at the Saks outlet store."

"Haba Amaka, Igbo woman, always looking for the bargain."

"Of course, why not?" she smiled.

She wasn't kidding either. She had just bought a fixer upper in Grant Park, rehabbed the kitchen and the bathroom herself and the place not only looks like something out of a home magazine but it has appreciated in value by $40k. The babe will make someone a solid wife someday.

In fact, I don't know what her problem is; guys are always interested but she is romantic to a fault. I've known her for ten years and in all that time I think she has had maybe one real relationship but several flirtations. She can't seem to get past the sweetheart phase, when you are both infatuated with each other. She keeps dreaming about her prince charming. He has to be tall, handsome and polished, and he has to be Igbo.

Actually, the real problem with Amaka is that she is so focused on pleasing everybody, especially her mother. It's so crazy, here she is thirty years old and her mother still has so much control over her. The woman calls her at all hours of the day, forever demanding to know all sorts of things, like if she is still dieting, has she gotten a pay raise at work, has she found a suitable man to marry. I tell you, she has Amaka going round in circles so that any man she meets not only has to live up to Amaka's idea of romance, but has to meet her mother's criteria too. Not only does she have to find a romantic African man that she connects with but he has to be Igbo as well. My sister, that's like saying you want a fabulous designer dress for under $50. You may find one, but you'll have to search long and hard.

Speaking of men, there was one fine brother checking Amaka out and who could blame him! My girl was looking rather hot, the bronze against her velvet skin and her hair down in loose waves. Even I was checking her out! Anyway, the guy was particularly fine and new on the scene; I had never seen him before. He was about 6' 4" and a cross between Will Smith and Boris Kodjoe, in a good way that is, so at least he met one of Amaka's criteria. He smiled at us and raised his glass since we had all turned and were so obviously checking him out. I raised mine back, Amaka looked away and Mina, well, she smirked.

Mina's husband, Obinna, came over and took his protesting wife onto the dance floor. She couldn't flow with the music because she was obsessing about her Vera Wang; she didn't want any of *"these clumsy oafs to step on her train."*

Meanwhile, I saw Dele alone and decided to go and corner him. I felt a little guilty about leaving Amaka but I turned around and saw Mystery Man had sauntered over and was trying to put it on her. *Get him girl, get him and if you no want, I fit collect?*

Amaka

Chemistry

I couldn't believe how amazing that Nouveau Africana party was. I don't know how it happened but I really enjoyed myself. Usually at these things I end up sipping on a glass of wine all night, watching Mina and Titi have all the fun. Titi usually has her pick of men and Mina, well, she has Obinna. As for me, I am usually the brown girl outside the ring; in fact I am the brown girl fading into the wallpaper.

I really hate being alone, but what can I do? I don't have Mina's elegant looks or Titi's sex appeal. I am just a regular Naija girl. Okay, I'll admit; I am on the plumper side of regular. Mina keeps giving me diet advice and Titi insists that I am fine as I am; all I need is a little more confidence. I never used to worry about marriage, I just knew that God was in control and his time was best. But over the years, as 30 came closer and closer, I found my life changing and my faith eroding. I haven't been to church in ages and well, let's just say things have changed.

My mother apparently thinks I need intense prayer and fasting and that I also need to stop being so picky. She keeps sending me these emails advising me to go on these dry fasts to coincide with some prayers that this or that potent prayer group is doing. She drives me crazy! Add to that her constant questioning through phone calls and text messages and crazy set-ups that she keeps denying and you have the stuff of a laugh out loud comedy, except I'm not laughing.

I mean, take for instance, this phone call and tell me how you would feel if your own mother thought this would be a potential mate. The call went exactly like this…

"Hello?" I said.

"Ha-low," a voice said in a very heavy Igbo accent—mind you, I don't particularly have a problem with heavy accents, it's just that the men I meet with them are usually just as parochial in their thinking.

"How are you?" he said, interrupting my thoughts.

"Fine," I said a little impatiently. "Who is this?"

"You don't know me, but my name is Festus and I am looking for a partner."

Needless to say the conversation went downhill from there. He informed me that he was currently working as a probation officer or something but his big claim to fame was that he was studying to be a nurse and he didn't fail to tell me, "You know I can make a lot of money working overtime!"

My mother just doesn't understand what I want. She thinks I should be happy with any man, just as long as he is Igbo and hardworking. She totally knocks the ideas that I have of meeting someone who is polished enough to move in any circle, Igbo or otherwise; someone who would enjoy Broadway as well as read Chinua Achebe. I mean the only way the men she keeps sending to me relate to Chinua Achebe is that they could be one of the traditional chauvinists in his books. As for Broadway, please -- as far as they are concerned, that is just some street in New York.

It's so crazy. All my life my mother tried to expose me to the finer things: tennis lessons at Ikoyi club, piano recitals and so on, and now because I have just turned thirty, she wants me to marry the first Johnny just come.

The truth is that there was one guy that I felt that I loved enough to spend the rest of my life with -- Kwame Wilson. I met him years ago at the African students' conference. He was studying at Harvard. The first time our eyes met, I had no idea who he was; but I just knew that we would become part of each other's lives. By the end of the weekend, we had become fast friends. We exchanged phone numbers and email addresses and over the rest of the semester we bonded over shared experiences as immigrant students in America: the stupid questions people asked about Africa, the racism and the new culinary and social experiences.

Kwame wasn't handsome in the traditional sense of the word, but he was very attractive, a man who was very comfortable in his own skin. He drew women to him; he was like Godiva to chocoholics.

Our romance began when we spent a summer together in New York, where I was doing an internship at *Gourmet* magazine and he was doing a program at the Columbia School of Public Health. That was the summer I first fell in love. He used to come over to my little studio apartment in Brooklyn and I would cook him egusi or jollof rice, occasionally he'd bring Ghanaian delicacies like kenkey or banku. We would talk about our dreams and aspirations.

One day after dinner, we were lying on the roof of his building. He had sublet this apartment for the summer which wasn't much to write home about, but it had a great rooftop deck. That night we had packed a picnic basket, a portable CD player and a bottle of cheap wine. We felt so cosmopolitan. I was only about twenty and he was twenty two.

After eating, we lay down on a mattress and gazed up at the sky, listening to a Bob Marley CD. We had come to a lull in the conversation and the song that had been playing came to an end. I still remember that moment like it was yesterday. He turned to me and said, "Do you know what I have wanted to do all night?" His voice was low and gravelly.

"What?" I asked innocently, because even though I was not unaware of the sexual tension between us, I was simply content to be next to him, the evening could not have been more perfect.

"I've wanted to kiss you."

I remember noting how fast my heart was beating, that I had begun to feel a little light-headed. It was a different time then. We had spent practically every evening together for about two months and the summer was coming to an end. He never made a move and being a virgin, I definitely didn't make any moves. I didn't know what to say, I just looked at him. He must have taken my expression as an invitation because he kissed me.

I feel like there should have been drum rolls or a symphony playing even now, because even that could not describe how wonderful that kiss was. It was everything I thought a kiss should be. That night, for the first time, I put aside all my fears and thoughts of my parents' disapproval and gave in to the sensation of pleasure and love. Kwame was my first and at the time, I thought he would be my only.

When the summer was over, we started a long distance relationship, he in Boston and me in Bronxville, NY.

Things changed soon, when my mother decided that a liberal arts education was a waste of my time and I should focus on getting a practical degree, like medicine or pharmacy. She announced over the telephone that she had decided pharmacy was best and that I should study in Boston, where my aunt and uncle could keep an eye on me. I went without argument, partly because I believed that it was futile, but also because it would bring me closer to Kwame.

When I moved, our relationship shifted into high gear. We became incredibly close. I met his parents and siblings but I never introduced him to mine. He was always a little bothered by that. Every time the subject came up, we would argue. I tried to explain that my mother was very opposed to me being with anyone who wasn't Nigerian. He couldn't believe that I didn't have the courage to stand up for myself.

When he graduated from his program at Harvard, I sat in the audience next to his mother, who had been smiling at me all day. That night after dinner with his parents, we sat in the lobby of their hotel and he put his arm around me. I snuggled into his chest.

"I am moving to London," he said. "I've been offered a job there that will take me closer to where I want to be."

I looked at him. London was so far away.

"Come with me, Amaka."

I was in shock. "You expect me just to pack up and move? My parents would have a fit."

"Not if you were moving with your husband." Kwame smiled. He produced a ring. It was beautiful, antique style. "It is my mother's, we have her blessings."

My mind was in turmoil. I loved him, but this relationship had been for me like a fairy tale, like a beautiful fantasy, and real life was where my mum lived. I didn't think the two worlds could coexist.

Kwame saw the turmoil on my face and said, "You don't want to marry me?"

I couldn't speak, but tears started to well in my eyes. His eyes darkened and his body became rigid. I've always wondered if the muscles of the heart harden as well. He took his arm away from me.

"I never thought it was real, this obsession with marrying a Nigerian man, but I guess it is. I wish for once though you would be honest and admit that it's not your mother's obsession, it's yours!" He stood up angrily. "I really cared for you," he said slowly. Then he turned and left.

I wanted to call out to him but I didn't. At first I almost felt relieved; I had been walking this line that I knew I didn't have the strength to cross. But for months later I was still brought to tears whenever something reminded me of him. I would look out of the bus window and remember us walking down that street and realize that I would never feel his hand over mine, his rough skin holding mine tightly as we crossed the street.

The summer months afterward were the hardest. I had no friends, no life, and because I felt so badly about what had happened, I avoided everyone we both knew. Every now and again we would bump into each other at odd places. It was the hardest thing, my heart would start beating fast when I recognized his walk and in the moments before he saw me, I would fantasize that we were like before and then he would look up and notice me and frown or walk the other way.

It is a crushing feeling when you recognize that you are still in love with someone who has come to hate you. I was torn between a sense of deep loss and a sense of duty, caught between sorrow and relief. I don't know how I got over him. One night I cried until the sun came up.

That summer went by in a blur and I threw myself into my studies the next semester. I couldn't sleep or eat and it took all my energy to study. It was a hellish semester but at the end of it, one day I realized it was over. It took a while to get over him, but I have. I heard he is married now and lives in New York.

Since then, I have never had a real relationship. Mere flings, but my one rule has always been that they had to be Igbo. In reality, it has been very hard to find the sort of man that attracts me and who is also Igbo in this vast country. So as you can imagine, I was quite excited to go the NA gala, a place where polished African men were sure to be found. And so the night before the party I decided to take Titi's advice and find my inner diva.

It all started with the dress. I wouldn't normally wear a dress quite like that, one that showcased all my curves. But Titi was insistent that it looked fabulous on me and since, in her words, my curves actually look nice, the idea was that I should show them off. I decided to go with the look, with good results I think. Even Mina said I looked decent and coming from Mina that was high praise. Some people can't understand why I am so close to Mina; I guess you really have got to know her to love her. The girl is truly good-hearted but she is continually putting up a façade for the world.

Anyway, I put on the dress and I discovered that I actually felt sexy. I had soaked in a bath with these Bvlgari bath salts that Mina gave had given me for my birthday and then I had put on my Syleena Johnson CD and sang with major attitude to '*Guess What*' as I did my hair. I put on my makeup – well, just mascara and lip gloss and a hint of eye shadow. I don't wear much makeup and fortunately people say I don't really need to. Then I got dressed and put on these sexy Jimmy Choo sandals.

Shoes are my one weakness. I may be fairly simple when it comes to my clothes but I love seeing my feet encased in pretty shoes. After all of that preparation, when I looked at the finished product in the mirror, I was amazed to see that I looked and felt pretty hot. In fact, as Titi put it, I was practically sex on legs!

I gave my hips a little wiggle and by the time I got into my car, I was sure that since I was feeling good and looking fabulous, I was going to have a great time at the Gala.

The party was happening as predicted; everyone who was everyone was there. I even saw that Nigerian model who is making waves these days and that sexy Yoruba actor from that HBO show.

Although the actor that really does it for me is that Chiwetel Ejiofor. The man is so sexy in a subtle kind of way. I saw him again in my favorite film, *Love Actually,* and I practically kissed the screen. Plus he's Igbo as well. If only...well, a girl can dream, can't she?

About half an hour into the party I could feel my high evaporating. I was beginning to feel like I usually feel at these things -- like a wallflower. I mean there I was, standing there next to bombshell Titi, who was giving even the models a run for their money in her red dress and Miss Perfection, Mina, who gave new definition to the word coiffed, not a hair out of place and her designer gown fitting just so.

All of a sudden, I started to feel less voluptuous and more fat. The curves that I had felt hot with were starting to feel more like extra rolls. If only I could listen to my mother and stick to my diet. I was chastising myself for eating that extra bagel this morning when this guy walked up to me. He looked like someone out of a magazine. Just beautiful! All I could think as he walked up was *"so out of my league."*

He had that whole soulful thing happening with his eyes. He was truly handsome. When I looked up and saw him coming towards us, I assumed he was going for Titi. I mean she is a stunning woman. Just the right shade of brown, in great shape, which I guess comes from working out an hour a day every day. Her abs are completely flat and she is all tits and ass. Naturally she is a hot commodity with the guys.

Unfortunately, I don't think they see her as quite marriage material— that is the kind of guys she wants anyway. The problem with Titi is you can see her desire for a rich man from a mile away and what man wants to feel like all he is a dollar bill to his woman, even if *it is a hundred dollar bill.* I keep telling Titi to focus on getting a good man, but she always counters by telling me to focus on getting a man -- period. I always laugh, although sometimes I wonder if I'm ever going to find anyone.

Then Jeffrey walked into my life. It was a made for a movie moment. The people around us began to blur and the room started to get dark and all I could see was him. By the time I realized that he had asked me to dance, I was in his arms and they felt so good.

They felt strong, not like a body builder's arms, but like a real man's should feel. They were playing Mary J. Blige's song, "Be Without You" and we were slow dancing. I found myself feeling all sorts of crazy things for this man and all I knew was his first name. I could feel his hands around the small of my back and he was holding tight enough for me to feel him and yet it wasn't intrusive. When the song was over, we walked out into the lobby.

We started to talk and he told me that he had just moved here from Nigeria and he was doing a sabbatical at Remore Law School. He said he had a practice in Lagos but things weren't going as well as he would have liked so he was rethinking his strategy.

He told me he was in his late thirties and still felt like he had never really been in love. I told him that I worked as a pharmacist but secretly desired to be a world class chef. I told him that I was sick of men seeming one way and turning out to be another. He told me how at thirty-eight, he had decided to become true to himself. I told him I didn't know if I still believed in love. He told me that he lived for it.

We talked till the music died down and people were getting their coats to leave so we moved to the hotel bar. Titi and Mina came by to say goodnight. Titi gave me the thumbs up gesture behind his back and Mina simply pointed to her watch. We talked till the night started to become the morning. By then I think I was already in love.

I only knew what he told me, but I felt like I knew him well. He was from one of those fairly well-known families in Lagos. He was Igbo like me but spoke Yoruba fluently and was what you would consider a Lagos boy. He had the typical pedigree: King's College secondary school, university in England and then back to Lagos for law school.

He was sexy, smart, and polished to perfection. He held my hands and played with my fingers. He told me that I was amazing, that he found me attractive, very sexy; he confessed that he really wanted to book a room for the night and invite me to share it with him.

I said nothing because my throat had become so dry and besides, I couldn't trust myself. I knew that if he pulled me into his arms right then and there, I wouldn't have the strength to resist. I was looking at his lips as he talked; this man was beautiful. He turned me on with his words as well. I mean he made me feel like I was the only woman worth knowing. He told me that he had never had a conversation like this with anyone, and that I really got him and he felt for the first time in his life like he had made a real connection. He said he thought that he finally had a small understanding of the word soul mate.

While we were talking he saw a friend who he knew in the hotel bar and excused himself to go and talk to him. I peered at him over my wine glass as I sipped my Riesling. He was really something. I was getting myself into trouble; I started to feel a wave of panic welling up inside of me.

What was I doing? My thoughts were conflicting. "This isn't you, what are you going to do, sleep with him tonight?" I shivered as I thought about what the night might bring. "No!" my mind responded, "It's got to be perfect. Is he perfect, is he your prince?" I looked over at him walking back to me, his long legs striding confidently over the sage and gold carpeting with his tuxedo jacket showcasing his strong broad chest. As I savored the image, he caught my gaze and smiled. I drifted in his eyes and smiled then I answered my earlier question, "he just might be…"

Mina

The good life

I can't believe Amaka stayed back with that guy, Joshua or Jeffrey or whatever his name is! She can be so stupid. She barely even knows that man and she is probably going to sleep with him. How can she be so naïve? She'll probably fall for the first line he throws out. The truth is that men that good looking don't go for women like Amaka. He can only be interested in sex for one night.

Anyway even if he were interested in more, she wouldn't know how to handle him. If it were me, I would have that man going in so many circles he wouldn't know which way was up unless I told him. I would never put myself out there like that; with men you have got to take control immediately or else you are finished. I guess I can't be too hard on her. It must be hard being a single African cosmopolitan woman over thirty, because the pickings are slim and you are competing with the young fresh ones.

As to be expected, I don't have to worry about that anymore. I am successfully married. People envy me -- married to a handsome, successful man. I live in a sought-after Atlanta neighborhood and my home can be called a mansion by any standard. I don't have to work for a living, so I have time for my other interests. Yes indeed, I am living the life I chose for myself.

People usually ask me how I got so lucky and I tell them luck had nothing to do with it. My life is good because I made the right choices. So many women out there make unintelligent decisions for stupid reasons. As for me, I wanted this life and so I knew what I had to do.

Take for instance, my husband, Obinna. When I met him, I was being chased by so many men but they were all the typical African professional man with an ego to boot. Obinna was a quiet and unassuming guy, but I already could see that he was going to make it. He was at medical school when I met him, brilliant but terribly unsophisticated. He was dreadfully uncultured. On my first visit to his apartment, he served me wine in a champagne glass, how gauche is that?

But I endured his lack of couth, why? Because I knew what tomorrow could bring. When I announced our engagement, Amaka gave me this whole lecture on passion and love. What has love got to do with it really? Frankly I am looking for security. Amaka, who is so focused on love and romance, where is she now? Single, over thirty and still hoping for Mr. Right! Meanwhile I am married to a very successful surgeon who has been featured in 'Who's Who in Black Atlanta' and quoted in *Atlanta* magazine.

I know I sound cold but that's the way the world works. After all, it's not as if I don't do my part for him. Like on the night of the Nouveau Africana Gala. He walked in with a woman like me: beautiful, slim, and elegant. He could have been single and looking desperately to mingle, like that poor Dan Okoli. Or even worse, he could have ended up with someone as crass and overweight as that Tigi Simpson. Furthermore, later on that night I let him make love to me.

The truth is I don't enjoy sex with my husband. He slobbers all over me and has no idea how to please me in bed. At best it's a clumsy effort at going down and at worst it's a sweaty attempt at *hitting it*, while I lie there praying for him to come already. Yes, clearly, Obinna doesn't do it for me. There is no chemistry for me.

So why did I marry him? Because I saw a man with potential, a man who was rough but teachable and I went for it, love be damned. And push him I did; when he was thinking about specializing, I pushed for surgery; when he wanted to do general, I pushed for cardiothoracic. I knew he had the brains and skills, he just lacked the motivation. I built him up. I buffed him and taught him about the finer things in life and every day, I push him just a little bit more.

Like with this house -- Obinna was reluctant to buy it, he felt it was really more than he could afford. I told him that one million five was really not too bad for a house;

after all, if he were in New York wouldn't he have to pay that just to live decently? He felt it was an unnecessary expenditure.

I disagreed. I know what I am used to and a swimming pool, eight thousand square feet, a gourmet kitchen with a subzero and Viking range just about brings me close. He told me he was thinking more about a three to four thousand square foot house, but who wants to live in a shoe box? Not me, I'm a woman who knows her worth and I am worth it. Decorating the house cost me quite a bit of money, but it looks divine. In fact one of the editors of *Atlanta Lifestyle* magazine called me, asking if they could feature our home. Of course, the answer was yes; after all, it is important that people see what true taste is, if only so they can have something to aspire to.

Now don't get me wrong, I'm not some lazy woman who sits at home eating bonbons. No way! Obinna is not the only one working hard. First off, I keep my body together. After four years, I can still fit into my wedding dress, which was a size two. So many women completely let themselves go once they get married.

I bumped into an old girlfriend in the grocery store and she looked absolutely horrific. She had gained at least thirty pounds, her hair was a complete mess, it looked like she hadn't seen the inside of a salon for months and she didn't have a stitch of make-up on and, my word, she really needed it. Mind you, this was a woman whose premarital wardrobe was like a designer sample sale and she used to have a standing appointment at Nseya, one of the hot hair salons in town.

I tell you honestly some women just don't try. It's like Amaka. Yes, she has a generous figure but with a little control she could probably be curvy like Beyonce or Halle or someone, but she refuses to control her eating. She is constantly eating rice or bread or something completely detrimental to looking good. It's not easy looking like I do as I forgo carbohydrates and spend hours in the gym but I don't mind, because I believe a woman should maintain her best assets.

Furthermore, while I may not have a traditional 9 to 5, I do work. I sit on several nonprofit boards and this allows me to hobnob with the crème de la crème of Atlanta society. Obinna and I have helped raise over one million dollars for various charities and organizations. My goal is to position him for public office one day; I can just see myself as a first lady. Maybe governor or maybe we will start small with mayor or something. That reminds me, I have to make sure we are invited to the Governor's Ball this year. I wonder who I have to schmooze to make sure that happens.

So as you can see, I work hard to maintain and make gains. I am no trophy wife; I am just a smart woman. My life is simply what I made it -- perfect! Well, almost perfect, the only thing that is missing is a child.

That's my only challenge and I am so frustrated. We tried for two years straight but nothing. We even went to a fertility specialist, which was difficult to begin with.

Obinna may be a modern man, but getting any African man to even contemplate the fact that he may not be shooting right at the target is complicated to say the least. He kept saying he was fine and if I needed to go I should but he wasn't going to be a part of it. Imagine the nonsense, a surgeon, a man who is medically educated, refusing to get himself checked out. What if it was his fault? Maybe his little swimmers were a tad lazy, so I badgered him until he agreed. Turns out, nothing is wrong with either of us, but it's just not happening. When I suggested IVF, Obinna flat out refused. It was the strangest thing. He felt the process was unnatural, which is so bizarre because I mean what's so natural about cutting into people's chests to sew pieces of their heart together?

Also there has been a new, strange development. It is as if he has lost interest in sex. Until last night, we had not been intimate in over six months. Initially when we first got together, Obi was always all over me, practically salivating when I walked into the room. I used to feign headaches and the like to put him off; I simply had no intention of sweating out my perm every couple of weeks. So initially he was thrilled when we started trying for a baby. He thought it would be sex all the time, any time. When I explained that I thought it was best if we concentrated on when I was definitely ovulating, he was a bit crestfallen.

But these days he barely notices me, just a perfunctory goodnight kiss on the forehead and then he is snoring. At first it was great because I really didn't need the stress of trying to dodge his advances, but now I am a bit concerned.

I know he is tired but my goodness, nothing is happening. Truth is I wouldn't ordinarily mind. The sex was never mind-blowing, just the same old, same old, steady and boring just like Obinna. But now, if I didn't know better I'd say he wasn't attracted to me anymore but that simply cannot be possible. Any man would be delighted to have me.

Like I said, I keep myself together; you should see my body naked, even my breasts are still perfectly rounded and perky. That's because I really watch what I eat, none of that heavy pounded yam and soup everyday. Obinna loves his local food, but it can wreak havoc on your body, and since I am not cooking two meals every night, he has gotten used to grilled chicken with vegetables.

I daresay my face hasn't aged either, thanks to the assortment of potions and creams I use daily. Ever since I read that Kimora Lee Simmons uses La Mer cream all over her body, I adopted that practice as well, and it works too because at 32, I don't have a single wrinkle or stretch mark.

That's why Obinna's inattentiveness really baffles me. If it were another man I'd be worried that he's getting his somewhere else, but the man is so dry, I just can't see him doing that. Anyway I am going to have to talk to him about it. If his libido is waning, maybe we can try some Viagra or something; or if nothing else, maybe he'll be willing to go the IVF route.

Something has got to give. After all in a few months, his mum is going to be visiting and I just cannot take any more of that woman's insults. She never liked me from the jump and she did everything to derail our relationship. Fortunately Obinna was too mesmerized by me to care about his mum's opinions. She felt I was just here to eat his money, which is not true. It's true I am not in love with Obinna, but I do care about him and plus I helped him get to where he is now. When I was dating him and he couldn't afford to take me anywhere decent, wasn't I managing then?

Honestly, she is your typical mother-in-law from hell. She criticizes my cooking, my way of dressing, even my manner of speech; she calls me 'oyibo.' She keeps saying that she is tired of tilling barren land, that if the land won't produce, then it's better that her son go and buy new land.

Meanwhile Obinna just stands there and says nothing. When we first got married, he used to stand up for me but these days he just shrugs his shoulders and tells me to endure it, after all I am not the first wife with a mother-in-law problem. Well, I am not leaving this marriage for some other woman to come and enjoy. All the work I did and some small girl will come and eat the fruits of my labor? I don't think so!

Titi

Another day, another dollar

I swear if I show another house to this ‘come today, come tomorrow’ couple, I will just scream. The man feels his level is around $300k, but the woman keeps making us see homes in the $500k range. But I even show them houses in the $600k range. I am no fool; I have noted the wife’s Vuitton purse and Cartier watch, while the hubby is in Dockers and Citizen. The kicker is that she’s a stay at home wife O! I tell you, monkey dey work, baboon dey chop.

Anyway, I have seen their pre-qualification papers and the guy makes fairly decent money and has great credit, so they can probably do around $700k in a pinch. Naturally the woman wants to live around the black gold coast in South Dekalb area. I showed them some of the decent subdivisions, like Water’s Edge and such, but Madam wanted to see the more moneyed places like Greenridge and even million dollar haunts like Sandstone and Belair Estates.

What's my own? Ask me and I will show you because the way I see it, this woman is going to force her hubby into a high priced home and cars and lifestyle, so while they qualify today, they'll probably be facing foreclosure tomorrow, but that's not my business. I'll still get my commission check so I'm totally with the wife.

In fact, today I showed them the ritzy Thurgood Estates subdivision. Starting from the $800's in Ellenwood, it was right up Madam's alley. She could just picture herself in the houses with the marble floors and the media room. She even asked the onsite realtor if they could put in swimming pools; I swear her husband farted in shock and boy, was it a stinker!

It was definitely one of those days and I'm just glad to finally be home and soaking myself in my garden tub. It's on days like this that I appreciate my condo. Sure it's not a ritzy 6000 square foot mansion, but it's cozy and comfortable for me. And one day, with the right man, I too will be pushing a loaded Range Rover while I ferry my kids to private school, and maybe I'll work for the fun of it, but until that time, I no dey craze, I work hard, and keep a little money away for emergencies.

I don't play with money. I have no intention of being poor. I know what poverty is. My mother used to sell roasted corn and groundnut on the streets back home in Nigeria. Fortunately I was pretty smart so I managed to get into the prestigious Queens Academy for secondary school, which is where I met Mina, although even she doesn't know that my mum used to sell local snacks on the side of the road. She thinks my mum was a business woman. Ok that's what I told her. It wasn't a lie! After all, selling roasted corn no be business?

As for my father, the man had like five or six wives and countless children, and I was so far down the food chain. You see, my mum wasn't even his legal wife, more like his concubine and I was her only child. When my mum died while I was in secondary school, I approached him for help with just the small school fees that Queen's Academy was asking for. He claimed he didn't know me and his wives chased me out of the compound with a broom. Afterwards he sent his driver to school with N200 for me. That couldn't pay even half of my school fees and besides I'm sure the man spent more on beer.

Anyway sha, I took the money; there is no shame when you are hungry. Thanks to my friend Chichi, I figured out a way to pay for my school fees and much more. At Queens Academy there were girls like Mina, who incidentally didn't really talk to me back then, who supposedly came from rich families and walked around with their noses in the air. And then there were the regular girls like myself and Chichi, trying to make a dollar out of 15 kobo. Actually there was a third group, the studious, dry ones, but who wants to hear about them.

Chichi was one of those girls in school that mothers call wild. At sixteen she had one of those attack and defense bodies. Decent sized boobs, small waist but an amazingly large ass. I am telling you, as she walked by in her school uniform you could see our male teachers lusting after her as they focused on the jiggle of her backside. And the girl used it to her advantage. I am not saying that she slept with any of our teachers; all I know is that she always got high marks in the subjects taught by men.

One day I was crying and worrying about the next semester, when Chichi came and sat next to me. When I told her what my troubles were she told me not to worry, that she had a solution, if I was willing to follow her lead. I didn't understand what she meant, but she soon showed me.

That weekend I left school with her on a pass and I learnt the meaning of bottom power. She took me to one party after outfitting me in shorts and a tube top with high heels. I wore make-up for the first time and I was surprised to see that I was really quite pretty.

At the party I met one Chief. This man was to become my provider for a fee. That night, he introduced me to another level of life. It was my first time and it was extremely painful but the fact that I was a virgin seemed to tickle the Chief and he tried to be gentle. He gave me N20,000 that night, enough to pay my school fees and more.

As the term wore on, I became his Saturday night regular and when I graduated and went to university, he put me up in a flat. I effectively became his property; I drove a brand new Honda and wore the finest clothes. Unfortunately, after some time, the honeymoon came to an end when his wife, along with some thugs, accosted me one day. They gave me a thorough beating and took the Honda, and she warned me to get out of Chief's life. I was in the hospital for a week and though he paid the bill, he didn't even come to see me. I was devastated. No one told me before I went and packed my things out of that flat and figured my next move.

Fortunately I had already been working on a plan B. I had also met this older man who worked for the US embassy and after a particularly hot and heavy session at a hotel, he had an attack of conscience and decided he wanted to save me from myself. He had promised to help me arrange for a US student visa and to help me get into a school so I could change my life. At the time I wasn't particularly moved by his request, but after the Chief fiasco, I took him up on it in a hurry.

Since then I have managed to work myself into the system here and find some relative success. I declared I was done with sugar daddies after that experience and I planned to make my own way, but I guess I have gotten used to the finer things in life, and so when I marry I don't see anything wrong in marrying up. I mean it's not like I plan on using the guy or anything -- I plan on loving him too.

There is just something about successful men that turns me on. Especially men like Dele. I mean he has the finesse and the wealth, not to mention that the guy is fine! The phone started ringing, just when I was about to start daydreaming about Dele and I walking off into the sunset. I hoped it was Madam calling to say she was ready to make an offer on one of the houses.

"Hello," I said sweetly into the phone.

"Titi," a gruff voice that I knew all too well barked into my ear.

"Yes," I replied, putting some distance in my voice.

"Why are you acting like you don't know who this is?"

"Segun," I said, pretending to be interested.

"Ehen, who else or are you seeing any other guys?" he snarled.

"I beg, sweetheart, give me a break; after you I no go fit," I said sweetly.

"You know it," he said, sounding smug.

Segun was one of the guys who had helped me get on my feet when I first moved to the States. He is a flashy guy who has no visible source of income but lives incredibly large, drives a nice car, spends a lot of money (in fact most of the designer bags in my closet are gifts from him) but doesn't work. I won't lie; Segun is the kind of guy that does deals. Shady, dirty 419 type deals. Credit card fraud, bank check fraud -- you name it and he's into it.

When I first came, I needed so much help, I didn't care where it came from. He saw me and desired me, so we both got our needs met. I was his girl and he took care of me. He bought me my BMW, cash down; he gave me a substantial down payment for my condo. To be honest, he financed the life I'm living.

The problem is that now that I am trying to upgrade to a different class of men, and the dude won't leave me alone. I haven't accepted a gift from him in at least a year; well, if you ignore the diamond earrings and necklace he gave me for Christmas. I couldn't resist, plus I knew I was going to the gala and I needed those pieces to complete my look. So what if it cost me a rough ride in bed?

Yes O, Segun is one of those guys that likes everything rough. I have never enjoyed sex with him. He is all about the blow job and hitting it from way back. Heck, I think he's a closet homosexual.

I have tried to shake him but I have to be careful about it. Last year, I tried to break things off with him and he stalked out of the house. The next night I was opening the door on my way out and he showed up out of nowhere, pushed me in and held a knife to my throat. His eyes were red and he looked crazed or high actually. "Bitch, you don't leave me till I am done with you." After that, I didn't quite know what to do but I knew I had to tread carefully.

Fortunately he is only ever around for short stints, then he has to go underground again. So I might not hear from him for months when he's gone and his time with me usually lasts about a couple of weeks. He is definitely a chapter in my life I wish I knew how to close.

"So what are you doing?" he asked.

"Taking a bath," I said.

"Good, because I like you fresh and clean," he laughed loudly.

"O-kay," I sighed.

"Come and open the front door for me, I'm outside," he demanded.

"Alright, give me a minute to get dressed."

"No, come as you are, dripping and everything!" he retorted sharply.

"Segun, it's cold, I don't want to get sick," I pleaded. I could only imagine if one of my neighbors was in the hallway.

"Titi, don't make me wait out here one extra minute," he ordered.

"Ok, ok, I'm coming." Oh shit. It's going to be a long, hard night.

Amaka

I keep on falling

Jeffrey was all I could think about since I had met him. I was hopelessly infatuated. He appeared to be everything I wanted: tall, handsome, Igbo, intellectual, sexy and he wanted me. That was the icing on the cake.

He was the kind of man I had always thought was out of my league. I remember when we were in college, Mina was considered the fine one; Titi, the sexy one and I was just there. Well actually, I was the goody, goody one. That's what Titi and Mina would call me. They would whisper to themselves about things they would do with their boyfriends; of course, I didn't have one and was telling anyone who would listen that I would be a virgin until I got married. Titi and Mina would roll their eyes in irritation when I said that; still they took me like their little naïve sister and that kind of hasn't changed. I don't mind. I never had any sisters before.

Actually on campus they used to call us the Nigerian sisters, because we were always together after class doing strange African things–their words, not ours. We used to act crazy and crack each other up, like that day in our dorm lounge. We used to stalk the lounge because that was where the TV was and on the days that the black TV shows aired, back then only *A Different World* and *The Cosby Show,* we would camp out. We had to make sure that none of the other students got to the TV before we did, to watch MTV or something dreadful.

So this particular day, we were waiting for our shows as usual and I had just finished drinking a can of coke. Instead of throwing it away, I began to tap it with a fork: ting, tin, tin, ting, tin, tin, tin, tin. And then Titi started drumming on the coffee table: ba da ba, ba da ba, ba da ba, Mina joined in singing loudly: 'Omo mi ma soun ere' and then we joined in with the chorus to that popular Christy Essien song. We sang for a while at the top of our lungs. I guess we were really homesick, being the only Nigerians on campus. Other students walked by and looked at us strangely. One of the girls asked us to stop making noise, telling her companion that we were probably doing some African ritual. Of course, this only made us crack up and sing louder.

Before you could say Jack Robinson, the resident director was commanding us to stop and come into his office. There he proceeded to ask us why we were making such a racket. We said for no reason. That didn't satisfy him and, apparently, he felt we were behaving very erratically, because the next question he asked was whether we were on drugs. We laughed even more heartily at this suggestion. Drugs were unnecessary, we were high on life. He turned red at our laughter and obviously felt slighted; he was going to write us up for creating a disturbance. We were already almost on probation because of a phone scam we had pulled but that is another story, so we couldn't afford to let him write us up. So naturally Mina and Titi seduced the geeky little fellow with promises they never intended to keep and soon all talk of writing up was forgotten.

Obviously, I was not the one known for my prowess with men, so when a man like Jeffrey comes my way, it always floors me. He sent me this lovely bouquet of orange roses and invited me out for dinner on Monday. Naturally I accepted. You know, I don't usually let down my guard with men, but there's something about this guy. I can't lie, I've been dreaming about him every moment since.

I got up really early Monday and looked at myself in the mirror. It was like looking at a different woman. Was my life going to be the same after today? I got dressed as I usually do, but today I put on a pretty blouse and trousers. I got made up; usually I hit work *sans* makeup, just moisturizer and lip balm. I smiled throughout the day. Nothing could bring me down. Not the ghetto girl who told me to go back to Africa because I wouldn't give her a narcotic medicine that the doctor hadn't ordered; not the crazy white guy who called me an uppity black bitch; not the druggies, the welfare chicks, the pushy patients who wanted their prescriptions called in their way, right away.

I walked through the day in a haze. I checked every drug order three times, because I couldn't concentrate. At exactly 5 o'clock, I said good night to everyone. I couldn't care less that the number of people waiting for their prescriptions seemed to have grown exponentially. They were just going to have to manage without me. I was going to meet my man!

I drove home in record time. Somehow the I-285 that always crawled with rush hour traffic was clear, even the roads were giving way to my romance.

I took a shower, curled my hair and then shook it out till it fell in soft cascading waves around my shoulders and down my back. I sprayed on my perfume and channeled Carrie a la sex in the city. Never mind Carrie is a blond wasp from New York, today she was dark, voluptuous and Naija.

Jeffery called and said to meet him at Babette's Café, a French restaurant in Atlanta noted for its romantic ambiance and good food. I got there just in time, and he was already waiting. Looking incredibly good in chocolate slacks and a chocolate cashmere pullover, with chocolate loafers, this man had style.

I was so glad I had put on my dark rinse Dolce & Gabbana jeans, a find in a size 14. These jeans make my hips and thighs look more Beyonce and less Monique. I topped it with a bustier style camisole and tie front cardigan. As soon as he saw me, he started to walk towards me. I tried my best to walk extra sexy in my Casadei stiletto booties, which I'd found on clearance from bluefly.com.

When I was close enough, he pulled me into his arms and kissed me on my mouth. If the date had ended right there and then, the kiss would have been enough. Good lord, I don't know where I found the self-control to act like a lady and go into the restaurant and start and finish the date. We walked in and were immediately seated.

Jeffrey perused the menu like a pro, and then when the waiter came he conversed easily in French. He ordered in French and even picked out the wine to go with our meal. It was an exercise in elegance, even though I knew that it was probably all for my benefit. If Titi were here she would be chanting "Effects!" It was so obvious he was clearly trying to impress me with his sophistication. I knew his moves were probably game; but good lord, I wanted to play.

We talked about everything under the sun: politics in Nigeria, love in America and yes, sex. He seemed to be amazed at the easy way I spoke about sex. According to him, most girls he knew acted all 'holier than thou' when it came to sex. I smiled because that used to be me.

In fact I was a virgin until age twenty three. I know, either way it's crazy. To have held out that long, or to not have held out until marriage like I planned. Well, such is my life, stuck in the middle and you know what's crazier? I didn't give up my virginity to some man I thought was the love of my life. No, it was some random dude I dated for a short while after college.

I had become so conflicted about my faith and everyone I knew was doing it, even some members of the church I used to attend. I just felt like I was behind and backwards and just wanted to get it over and done with. So I did and it was so anticlimactic. Funny thing is that I had sex to become a woman, so to speak; but after the fact, I felt like I lost myself. I lost my faith, well somewhat, anyway. I mean I believe in principle, but I don't know if you could say I am living as a Christian.

Ok, can I be completely honest? I can't believe I'm admitting this but well, when I looked over at Jeffrey, I was glad I had rid myself of any such restrictions, because clearly a man like him would not have a relationship where sex wasn't involved and I was so ready to have a relationship with him.

He told me about his business in Nigeria. He had set up a law practice and was dabbling in oil and gas. Clearly he had been quite successful, but his present sabbatical was not just to further his intellectual education but to take a break from the life he had and explore new options. When he said that he had a twinkle in his eye and reached over and touched my hand and that was when the conversation really got hot and heavy.

At some point during the evening, after Jeffrey had fed me pork tenderloin and chocolate bread pudding with his fingers, I felt for certain that this was all just raps. I mean the romance factor was through the roof. I banished the thought as soon as it came, because truth be told, I no longer cared -- the whole thing felt so damned good. We were having such a wonderful conversation and I had had a little bit of wine, actually I had stopped counting after the third glass. We didn't notice the restaurant emptying out, until the maître d' came over to ask us if we would be much longer. I looked around, no one else was there and the staff was actually clearing tables. Jeffrey immediately settled the check and left a hundred dollar tip.

It had been such an intoxicating night that when we got up to leave, I could barely manage my stilettos, let alone my car. So he did what any gentleman would do. He drove me home. I was not too far gone to notice that he drove a very nicely set up Range Rover. I nestled into the plush leather and started to drift off as we listened to music. Thankfully he had a navigation system and didn't need any directions from me.

Soon we arrived at my house and I vaguely remember him walking me to the house, but as I leaned into him, I remember thinking that his cologne smelt citrusy. He took me to my bedroom, took off my boots and my cardigan and laid me in my bed. After which I drifted back to sleep and dreamt of weddings on the beach.

Mina

Porous brains

I just don't know how some women can be so foolish. Imagine my friend, Katya, allowing some young Caribbean girl to come and be a nanny in her house. How can any reasonable woman take petrol and matches and put them in the same place and then start complaining when a fire breaks out?

Katya's problem is that she is biracial. Her mother is German and her father is Nigerian and so somehow she thinks the rules don't apply to her. She and her husband were married a couple of years ago and have a baby. Now, of course, Katya has a solid career in finance. She is a VP at Citibank. One of several I know, but still she is doing pretty well. Her hubby is a lawyer. Well, he was a lawyer, but recently he decided that he wanted to take some time off to pursue his passion which was writing. So this man, who just had a baby and has all these bills to pay, because naturally they have a hefty mortgage and the car notes on the S class and the M class are no jokes either, decides that he needs to take the time off now.

Katya was, of course, pissed off. But she felt like she couldn't do anything about it; her baby was only a couple of weeks old at the time and she didn't have the energy. If Obinna tried that passion nonsense on me, I would have taught him that his passion better be making money, just like my passion is spending it. Baby or no baby, when your house is on fire, you better have enough energy to douse it, otherwise, you might find yourself sleeping on the streets!

Anyway back to the story, so she carries herself back to work after four weeks. Can you imagine the girl wasn't even completely healed; but you know, since her hubby wanted to play author and she was stupidly trying to be the supportive wife, she had to go back to work. So of course she was desperate for childcare. She went through a nanny referral service.

When she saw this Rihanna girl's resume, it was amazing. It was as if the girl was Mary Poppins re-incarnated and her references were excellent. So she ignored the fact that the girl looked like she just stepped out of a music video. Actually, the day I saw her she was wearing shorts and a tank top. As soon as I saw her I told Katya to fire her, because no matter how attractive you are, you should never put a competitor in your house; but of course Katya didn't listen. She told me I was being a paranoid Nigerian. So I left her alone – her, her passionate husband and her shorts wearing nanny.

Naturally when she called me today after several months, somehow I was not surprised she was in tears. Apparently her husband had been having writer's block and somehow Rihanna decided to inspire him by opening her legs. Did I not warn Katya? I knew it. Hot pants my foot! Anyway, bottom line is that Rihanna has just informed them that she is pregnant by Katya's husband and fully intends to keep the baby.

So now Katya is basically screwed and because her idiot husband isn't working, if they divorce, she might end up paying him palimony, imagine that! Her baby has just started crawling and this happens.

I was too disgusted, and even more so when I talked to Katya and she said her life is in God's hands. I am telling you, I am sick and tired of people being too weak to face life and hiding behind God. It's not like I don't believe in God, it's just that I don't see what place He has in my life. I don't need him. I have everything under control; I am not stupid like Katya. So when she started spouting this church jargon, talking about "No weapon formed against me" and all that, I told her to get real and I referred her to Titi to help her find a new place and called a few friends of mine for a referral to a good divorce lawyer.

Honestly, women and their porous brains, how can you take trouble and put it in your house? That is why in my house, there will never be any drama because I know how to handle my life and I make sure it is handled.

Katya kept crying to me about how she loved him and she couldn't believe he could do this to her and all that. I was so irritated. There was a point when I wanted to slap her. I mean why she was wasting her tears on that idiot, I'll never know. Imagine sleeping with the help, how cliché!

Months ago I warned her that she was being too soft on her husband. That catering to his every need would only make him take her for granted. Men are like wild animals. To get them to behave acceptably in public you have to use a little cruelty, otherwise they don't respect you.

Take for instance Obinna, he cannot try me, because I have him so trained that he is ready to jump through any hoop, just for a small tidbit of affection. I know what you all are saying, but that's okay, I've been called a hard bitch before and quite frankly, it doesn't bother me.

I learnt early on that the only purpose love serves is to make you feel bad; so as for me, I don't bother with emotions. I have always had a plan and I am willing to do whatever it takes to execute it. So say what you will, but you won't catch me with a hot pants wearing nanny. She better be old and grey with one lazy eye and even then I'll have my eye on the heifer!

Titi

How much?

One day I decided to indulge in my favorite pastime, shopping! I came to Phipps Plaza because it is the finest mall in Atlanta. All the high end retailers are here. From Gucci to Saks Fifth Avenue, I can get the latest fashion from the stores and might even see a celebrity or two. In fact, coming to Phipps Plaza combines my two favorite hobbies -- shopping and people watching.

Come and see babes. In fact, Atlanta babes do not play! Especially the African American ones, what! I can't lie O, these sisters take it to the next level. Every babe has a correct weave and is wearing some 'come and get me' high heels with a designer bag to match and then the outfit -- forget about it, it showcases the body to the fullest. In fact, what I like about Atlanta babes is that even the heavy ones, they too still try and let me tell you they are working it. They don't care that their stomachs are not flat, they are still out there rocking their curves and the guys are still checking them out too.

After I came to Atlanta and saw the way these babes handled business, I knew I had to step up my game; hence the constant shopping trips. Well, let me not lie, I have never needed a reason to shop.

This particular day I was eyeing the Fendi large calfskin B bag, but at over two thousand dollars, it was well out of my budget. Then I started thinking dirty; if I just had dinner with Dr. Dan, he would be so willing to buy this purse for me. I started to pull out my Treo to call Dr. Dan to set up a date for that night when I noticed one babe in a pair of tight jeans.

Actually the reason I noticed her was that she had one of those stripper bodies. She reminded me of my old friend, Chichi, all attack and defense -- a tiny waist and a huge butt. Her legs were big but very shapely and firm and she had very full breasts. She was wearing jeans and a blouse cut low that you could see her boobs and the fabric of her blouse was so thin you could see the outline of her nipples. I was still staring at her when I noticed the man she was with. It was none other than JJ.

He had his hand on her ass as usual and she was showing him a dress she wanted to try on. When she went to the fitting room, I walked over to him. The man was shameless. I mean I just received his wedding invitation, a beautiful ivory parchment with silk embellishment, the whole card hinted at how classy the wedding was going to be. They were getting married at the Georgian Terrace Hotel and were registered at

Sonoma Williams and Neiman Marcus; but I digress, back to this mess.

"JJ," I said, hoping to startle him, but he turned around smooth as silk.

"Titi, my love, how are you?" he asked.

"I should be asking you that question," I said.

"What do you mean?" he asked.

"I just received your wedding invitation and you are here palming Miss Stripper of the year," I said.

"You know she really is the dancer of the year. I met her the other night at Magic City and she does things with her stuff that you would not believe, plus she can make it clap, if you know what I mean," he said with glee as he reminisced. Dirty man!

"So?" I asked, "What about your fiancée?"

"What about her?" he said. "She can't make it clap."

Excuse me, but did this idiot just say 'make it clap'? Man, it's hard out here for a babe, catching a guy is not easy O! Gone are the days when all you had to do was look fine, now babes have to step up the game. I tell you, you have to be a professional woman, gourmet chef and have some serious stripper moves to boot. Make it clap indeed!

"Don't you feel bad cheating on her?" I asked, searching for one remorseful bone in his body.

"No, I don't. I love my fiancée, that's why I am marrying her, and by giving her my name, I am giving her access to my whole life for the rest of my life, but Peaches here is just a side dish. She knows it and I know it. In fact the way I see it, I would be doing my wife a disservice not to be with Peaches, because this way I get it all out of my system."

"Say what you will, JJ, cheating is still cheating," I replied.

"Then let it be cheating, because as for Peaches, maybe she'll get a little money out of me for it, but my wife will get it all," he reasoned calmly, flicking off an invisible piece of lint from his pants.

Let me not lie, at that moment I thought about adding "can make it clap" to my resume and if not for pride, I might have broken down and asked Peaches for a quick lesson.

Just then, Peaches came out of the dressing room, looking slightly obscene in short shorts and a halter top; in fact, one white woman took her child away while practically covering her eyes.

"You look delectable, my dear," he said.

She, on the other hand, only had eyes for me. She was eyeing me like a lioness eyes another lioness. I wanted to say, "Back up girl, you are so not on my level" but I chose the more cautious approach, silence.

JJ didn't introduce us, he simply gave Peaches a wad of cash and told her to go on and pay for it, because he wanted to get back to the hotel. She lost interest in me after seeing the wad of hundred dollar notes. While she went off to pay for her various items, I started to think of JJ in conjunction with my Fendi bag and even started to open my mouth to say something about it to him. Before

I could speak, JJ sidled closer to me and putting one hand on my hip, he whispered in my ear. "Now is there anything I can get for you?"

Immediately I cursed my earlier thought, because the bag might cost over two thousand dollars, but having JJ buy it for me would definitely cost me too much.

Amaka

Let there be love

I think I am in love. Jeffrey is amazing. First of all, that night, he laid me down in bed and then crashed on the couch like a true gentleman. The next morning I woke up to the delicious smell of sausages and eggs. He had made breakfast. He didn't have classes that day, so I did the only logical thing: I called in sick. For Tuesday and Wednesday!

From that minute we spent every waking moment together. We ate breakfast in my sunroom and it was perfect. You could see the chill in the air outside, yet we were warm and toasty inside.

After we ate, I cleared the dishes away. He walked behind me with a glass in his hand. I was loading the dishwasher when I felt his hand on my back. He pulled me to him and kissed my ear. I am not going to lie, shivers went through my body and I began to melt you know where. He kissed the side of my neck and then he lifted my hair and kissed the back of my neck. At which point I turned to him and offered my mouth. When his lips met mine, I can't explain what I felt, I don't know what happened; all I know is that I became so uninhibited.

I was so glad I was wearing my favorite piece of lingerie from Victoria's Secret. That morning when I woke up still in my jeans and realized that Jeffrey was in my kitchen cooking up some breakfast, I had put on the chemise and robe, fluffed up my hair, brushed my teeth and dabbed a little Jo Malone perfume where it counted. I wanted to have the 'I'm sleepy, what happened' look, but I wanted to look sexy. Boy, did it work!

We made love and it was wonderful. He moved smooth and slow and the foreplay was endless. It felt like warm chocolate was being poured all over me. In no time I was begging for the next level. He smiled and in one swift move, he took off his boxers and stood before me completely naked and looking glorious. What happened next almost brought me to tears. When we were finally together, it was like breaking the crust on crème bruleè. You don't know which is sweeter, the feeling of cracking the brown sugar or the anticipation of the sweet creaminess inside. Afterwards when he had called my name over and over and was spent, he pulled me onto his chest and we slept intertwined.

An hour later, I woke up to him stroking my skin. He smiled and said with a kind of awe in his voice, "Your skin is like silk." We never did make it out of bed that day.

We spent the next couple of days getting to know one another. We took in a play at the Fox and went by the Museum of Art. Jeffrey was cultured and educated. He spoke French, Igbo and even Italian fluently. We dined at Nava, danced at Sambuca and had drinks at Loca Luna. It was almost too good to be true. Unfortunately or fortunately, Thursday came along and I simply had to go back to work and Jeffrey had to get back to his apartment to catch up on some work.

Thursday went by in a blur of prescriptions and crazy people. It is funny how many people are mental in the United States. Titi calls them 'were a l'aso,' which means mad people wearing clothes. I mean you won't believe how many people came into my pharmacy acting crazy. I kept daydreaming about putting a double cocktail of Prozac and Valium into the water supply. Nutcases, at least back home in Nigeria, the crazy people roam the street naked so you know to give them a wide berth.

Tonight is girls' night. We should really make it Friday because it is so hard to make it into work after a night of wine and talking trash, but what can we do? Titi and I are single girls and we have to keep our Friday nights open. We usually meet at Mina's house because her hubby is on call and so we have an all-night gist session. Tonight was no exception, except Titi arrived a little late muttering something about getting rid of Segun. Segun, Dele, Ike, I can't keep up with Titi and all her men.

Mina had the place looking spectacular as usual. The formal living room was an ode to Africa, with wingback chairs re-upholstered in silk aso-oke, lime green with gold threads, providing a striking contrast to the chocolate suede sofa with gold piping. Original art adorned the walls; a beautiful oil painting by Bruce Onabrakpeya highlighted the east wall while sea green silk curtains framed the windows.

We sat in the family room where comfort met beauty. I settled into the rust colored oversized suede sofa and sipped the champagne she passed me.

"What are we celebrating?" I asked.

"Us, after all we are worth it," Mina said.

"Damn right, after all the suffer we dey suffer!" Titi chimed in.

"Ladies, to living, loving and being fabulous," Mina toasted.

"I heard that," Titi yelled, clinking her glass.

"Ditto," I cheered.

We had started the evening in high spirits.

"So, what's new and exciting in everyone's life?" Mina asked as she steered us to the kitchen where she had prepared dinner. No doubt something low calorie, low fat and, I hate to say it, low taste. It's sad, but in spite of her Le Creuset cookware, Viking gas range, subzero refrigerator, Hinckel knives, my Mina cannot cook. She has the best of everything. I love to cook in her kitchen when she lets me, just the stove alone puts me in heaven, but she is so rigid about everything that her food just doesn't taste good. My mother used to say "the key to cooking is the heart that cooks it," and Mina is a wonderful person but the girl has her heart locked down and passion is a dirty word where she is concerned.

Now since a sista has got to eat, I always bring a dish under the guise of "I tried something new and I want you guys' feedback." Titi's response is always the same: "Fantastic Maksy," which she calls me when she gets tipsy; Mina's is invariably: "Not bad, but a little oily for my taste." Today was no exception. I brought paella, chockful of seafood and meat. It was delicious if I do say so myself. Naturally Titi plowed through two plates of it while Mina munched on her tomato and basil salad.

After we had settled our stomachs, the gist began in earnest.

"Look O, before we go any further, me sha I must know the low down," Titi announced.

"What low down?" I asked, being coy.

"My friend, don't play with me! What is up with you and that beautiful fellow from the gala?" Titi asked.

"Oh, Jeffrey."

"Chai, you are in serious trouble; see the way she said it, 'Oh Jeffrey," Titi mocked.

"I know you didn't go home with him that night?" Mina looked horrified.

"Of course not," I insisted, "but I no fit lie, I almost did."

"Aha! You don knack the guy already! Bad girl!" Titi sang.

"Please O," I started to protest.

"Don't even try to lie here," Titi said. "I can see from your face that you have knacked the boy backwards and forwards."

"We did not have sex!" I spilt my champagne a little in my vigorous protest.

"Ehen, what did you do?" Titi challenged.

"We made love," I said, sighing dreamily.

"Ah ah, na wa O, love makers, I beg you knacked the boy jo!" Titi said triumphantly.

"It was the most wonderful experience I have ever had."

"So Jeffrey knows how to do the do?" Titi probed.

"I was once, twice, three times a lady O," I admitted.

"I hate to be the voice of reason here, but do you even know the guy?" Mina cut in.

"Mina, why are you always trying to spoil someone's show?" Titi asked. "Which one concerns you? Maksy is a grown woman, if she wants to knack, let her knack!"

"I said I didn't knack, this was more about the intimacy than the sex," I complained. I couldn't accept what Jeffrey and I shared being reduced to some tawdry act.

"Let me ask you something, did you have an orgasm?" Titi said.

"I already told you so."

"Then it was about the sex. Sure you like the guy but let's face it, you have only known him about what, a week? Me, I don't like to bullshit. Can you lay down your life for him; heck can you even give up something minor for the guy? Probably not, hence what you are feeling has less to do with love and everything to do with lust and as far as I am concerned, that's alright"

"I beg to differ. I think sex should be about something more than pleasure," Mina said. "It should be about the relationship, common goals and aspirations, aligned visions. You should at least know the guy's last name."

"I know his last name, thank you very much," I said irritably.

"No dey angry now, Maksy," Titi said. "I don't know what the big deal is about sex and Africans. We like to lie and get on our moral high horse, meanwhile the way HIV is spreading like wildfire, you know someone is knacking someone. The way I see it, let's get sex on the table and talk about it frankly."

"Ok, Madam Sex Therapist, talk about it," Mina said.

"Not a therapist, I'm more like a sex psychic. Like I can see that Maksy's been getting a lot of it and you, my darling Mina, ain't getting none. What's up with that?"

"Look, I'm a married woman and I don't think it's proper to discuss my sex life with you." Mina turned bright red.

"Since when? I beg I know that your old man's shekini curves to the right, so please save it."

"Who told you I haven't been having sex?" Mina said, her voice wavering.

"Well, it's easy enough to see," Titi or the champagne said. "You, my dear, are a classic case of frigid."

"I am not frigid. Just because I don't go around opening my legs to every man that can buy me a Gucci bag, that doesn't make me frigid."

"You know, Mina, I am so relaxed now that statement doesn't even phase me, and for the record, it's got to be at least a Chanel bag," Titi mused good-naturedly. "Anyway whether or not I am promiscuous, it doesn't change the fact that you are frigid, cold like ice. I know your poor hubby must be blue balling on the regular."

"Whatever, Titi," Mina said, getting up in irritation.

They started to argue in their usual way and I tried to be the peacemaker. This was how a lot of our gatherings went, but we always were able to smooth things over.

Today I diverted everyone's attention with a funny story I had with a customer in the pharmacy. I started mimicking the customer who had come into the pharmacy, a bonafide African-American princess. The kind that will ask you for your opinion on a drug and when you give it, will ask you to defend it. So that day, she was giving me a hard time as usual. Telling me in her clipped proper accent about how she had been reading a study about soymilk and premature puberty and what were my thoughts on it. I was preparing to give her my own brand of bullshit, when the guy behind her started to complain about her wasting time. Next thing my polished, Chanel suit wearing, Vuitton bag carrying, college educated customer, took it to a level I wasn't expecting. She just turned around and said: "Listen motherfucker, I am not the one right now, I am not the one!" Oh boy, after that the man kept quiet and I was blown away.

Titi and Mina were rolling when I gave them that gist and so we managed to get through their little tiff and have a fairly decent evening. But anyone could see the tension was just underneath the surface. Me, I left them quickly and as soon as I got in the car, I called Jeffrey.

Mina

Mummy on Demand

Honestly, that Titi, she really gets on my nerves sometimes. Imagine calling me frigid. Just because I don't go about shagging every man I see. Please, I have had enough sex to last a lifetime. What does she know? People just look at the surface and they think they know everything. Utter nonsense. I can't even begin to express how upset she made me. My husband blue balling, who is she to talk? Silly social climber! Who finds a good husband lying on her back?

That being said, I resolved to get to the bottom of this issue with my husband. Maybe he just needed to slow down at work. I decided to cook him a nice Naija meal. Maybe pounded yam and egusi stew, he likes egusi.

The phone rang while I was thinking.

"Hello," I said, picking up the gilt edged phone in the sitting room.

"Hello." A male voice and my blood ran cold. I was silent.

"Hello, hello?" he said more urgently.

"Yes?" My voice was like ice.

"Is this Mina?" he asked, like he didn't know my voice.

"Yes," I said like I didn't know his.

"This is Uncle Tosan"

"How are you, Uncle Tosan," I asked quietly.

"Very well thank you. Actually, I am in Atlanta on a business trip from Lagos."

I could only mutter in response: "Oh."

"Well, I was hoping I could see you; your mum gave me your number."

"I don't know if that is possible, Uncle" I said, silently cursing my mom. "You see, my husband and I are traveling."

"Oh. I see." There was a pause before he asked: "How is your husband? I hope he treating you well because you know you can just tell me and I'll make sure you are taken care of."

"Thank you, but that is unnecessary," I said. "My husband is a wonderful man."

"Mina, why so formal? It's me, Uncle Tosan. Don't you remember how we used to play when you were young? Remember the gifts, clothes and jewelry I bought for you?" he asked.

I did remember, I still have the one carat diamond pendant he gave me and I remember the day he gave it to me like it was yesterday. I don't have most of what he gave me, but I kept that piece, so I would always remember.

"I remember, Uncle," I said. "I'm sorry, it's just that you caught me at a bad time, may I call you back?"

"Sure, I am at the Ritz Hotel. Room 406."

Immediately I called my mother in Nigeria.

"What exactly is your problem?" I said as soon as she said hello.

"Are you crazy, young lady? Just who do you think you are talking to?"

"Mummy, for goodness sake, why on earth did you give Uncle Tosan my number?"

"Ah…because he asked for it?" she said. "What is the big deal?"

"I am married."

"So… it's not like he wants anything from you, just a little friendly conversation and you know he might finance you well for it.

"Mother, I am not a whore."

"Who is talking about prostitution?"

"You are. Besides I don't need to be paid for my conversation or anything else. My husband is rich."

"Oh really, well then send me the money I have been asking for."

"What money now?"

"Ehen, you are asking what money, useless girl. Other mothers have children who are buying them Benz's and

BMW's and you are asking what money. Is it because I don't make demands?"

I almost choked. Doesn't make demands she said. The woman texts me daily with details about what she wants me to buy and money I need to send for her essentials. Like the La Mer cream that I use, she insists that she must use it also, so that became part of her essentials. Every time she gets a wedding invitation, she needs a new lace outfit and a new bag and shoes to match and that is non-negotiable. I was looking at *Ovation* the other day and who did I see in the pages? None other but my mother, looking very fashionable in gold lace and her new Louis Vuitton that I had sent her, all on demand. My mother was a piece of work.

It's not like this comes as a surprise. Things are even better for me now that I am an adult. The woman loves money. She is the one that pushed me to choose wisely in marriage. I didn't even have the option of bringing home a man that I loved, unless that love presented itself in a thousand dollar suit and a bulging wallet. As far as she is concerned I married down with Obinna. "A common doctor" is what she says. Meanwhile the woman didn't even finish university.

My mum is what you call a senior chic. She never married. I don't know my father. Well, I know who he is and when I was younger, I used to tell people I was his daughter, until they started to rag me about the fact that I was never seen with him and most especially that I didn't bear his last name.

My father is one of the most well-known businessmen in Nigeria. He runs a huge conglomerate and has his hands in everything. He is always in the society pages because of one party or the other he is throwing. He had several children already and the funny thing is that I am the spitting image of them. In fact more than once, I have been asked if Tutu and Lolo, his two oldest daughters, who are well known for their events and PR business, were my sisters. When I was in secondary school I used to live for those questions but after a while they started to bring me down. His children lived lavish lives, and while my mother and I were not starving by any stretch of the imagination, it would have been nice to have some of the privilege that went along with being an Amakiri-George.

I'll never forget one evening in Lagos during the summer of my junior year in university. I was at Club Towers, one of the popular clubs at the time, as evidenced by the long line waiting to get in. My friends and I were in line when all of a sudden, this black Mercedes pulls up and out come these two beautiful girls with Robert Moji-Dabiri, a well-known actor. Everyone started shouting: "Robert, how now?" I looked at the girls, and there in front of me were Tutu and Lolo. My sisters! I pushed through the crowd and found myself practically in front of them. I looked right into Lolo's face. I searched her eyes for any signs of recognition. She looked right through me as if I was invisible. "Tutu, Lolo!" I heard Robert shout out, "come, this way, we can use the VIP entrance." As they were ushered in, the security guard tapped Tutu on the shoulder, he must have noted the resemblance, and asked, "Isn't she with you?" Tutu looked right at me. Then she shook her head. "I don't know that girl," and with a flick of her long hair, she walked into the club, while I was left outside.

After that I lost any illusions of belonging to the Amakiri-George family. I started to wish that my mother had chosen someone else to be my father. I wish she had given me a chance to be someone's legitimate child, but it is what it is and my mother is who she is. My mother knew exactly what she was doing when she went after my father. It was no tragedy of love. She knew he was married but pursued him because he was a handsome well-to-do man, and she, a student in university, had decided that the suffering was just too much. So she pursued him and got pregnant. When she had his child, she blackmailed him so he financed her house and her lifestyle, until the society pages got wind of it and then the shit hit the proverbial fan. His wife organized thugs to move us out of our home. I remember this because I was about eight at the time. My father came later to the flat where we were squatting to smooth things over, but my mother wasn't interested. She never felt for the man, all he was to her was a cash cow, and the cow had just been butchered.

That is when Uncle Tosan came into our lives. Uncle Tosan was about twice my mother's age. Older and richer than my father, and he didn't care if his wife knew about his affairs or not. He was known as a playboy.

He started coming around to the flat when I was going on ten. He would disappear into my mother's room and then reappear in the morning sometimes. As I got older, he started spending more and more time with us and our financial situation was upgraded in direct proportion to his favor.

He bought my mum a boutique which she still runs to this day. He bought her a Mercedes, a house and he paid for my American college education. However all these things came with a price, which my mother knew all too well and which I was about to find out.

Titi

Love for sale

Hallelujah! My 'come today, come tomorrow' couple finally showed up today and bought a house. A beautiful $900K home in Smoke Rise, Stone Mountain and it is even more beautiful when I think about my 6% commission. I am getting closer to my dream of starting my own company.

Oh, are you surprised? Of course, I have goals and aspirations; I just want a rich husband to go along with it. Me, I am an ambitious chick. I am not about to spend my life lunching at the garden club courtesy of my rich husband -- I am just trying to ensure that he doesn't bring me down. Plus I am simply more attracted to rich men. It's in the way they walk and talk. They know that they are correct, no need for TMY, too much yarn. Their confidence is so damn intoxicating for me.

Take for instance, Dele Thompson. Remember him -- CEO of Thompson Enterprises? Solid rich guy and fine to boot. I told you I saw him at the Nouveau Africana Gala.

Well, I managed to slip him my card that night and guess who calls me this morning. Dele Thompson. I no go lie, just hearing his sexy voice on the phone made me instantly moist. I beg don't act like you don't know what I am talking about, you goody two shoes. Hasn't a man ever turned you on so much that you can't control your response to him? That's what Dele does to me.

Anyway sha, the guy called me and I was too excited; but of course, I played it cool.

"May I speak to Titi Lawson?" He said in a deep, silky, upper crust British accent, with a hint of Naija.

"This is Titi Lawson, how may I help you?" I said breaking out my own phonetics.

"Hello, Titi, this is Dele Thompson," he said in a smooth drawl.

"Dele Thompson?" I replied, faking the funk.

"Yes, Dele Thompson," he laughed. "We both know you know who I am, but I'll play along."

"You know, I know I should know you but please refresh my memory," I said, determined to have the upper hand in this conversation.

"Well, let's see. You saw me at the Nouveau Africana gala, stalked me by the men's room and very blatantly gave me your card. Now do you remember?"

"Of course, Dele, how are you?" I said, laughing nervously; I couldn't believe he had called my bluff.

"You know we realtors, we have to be aggressive to be successful. Are you looking for a house?"

"So you want to sell me a house?"

"Of course, that's what I do."

"I was under the assumption that you were offering something else…"

I let that statement lie there for a minute. This guy was truly arrogant and full of himself, but I was still feeling him.

"Mr. Thompson, I see you are a very straightforward man."

"Well, I don't like to play games."

"Ok, well in all seriousness, what can I do for you?"

"Quite frankly, I found myself attracted to you, even though I typically don't go for women who pursue me and I would like to explore that. Also incidentally, I am in the market for a home."

"Well, you…"

"I want to take you for dinner." He asked, "What day is good for you?"

I hadn't even said yes and he was already trying to make arrangements.

"I'll have to check my schedule," I said as coyly as possible.

"You do that; my number is 555-1232. I'll be expecting your call."

Then he hung up. What an arrogant idiot! Why does he have to be so rich and handsome?

I was thinking about whether I should really go out with Dele or not, when the doorbell chimed. I looked out of the peephole and saw a man in a maintenance uniform standing out there. I had called for them to come and help me with my plumbing.

"Who is it?" I asked.

"My name is Emmanuel, madam; I am the new maintenance man. You said you had a problem with your plumbing."

"Ok, hold on," I said, opening the door.

"Thank you," he said. "Can you show me where the problem is?"

"Sure." I led him the guest bathroom. "The toilet is stopped up."

It was Segun that had blocked it. Since he was here last so many things had fallen apart.

As Emmanuel bent down to unclog the bowl, I noticed how strong he looked. His arms were muscular and bulging just a little bit. He appeared to have washboard abs and he was pretty good looking.

"Madam, you don't have to stay here, it might get a bit messy." I noticed a slight accent.

"Where are you from, Emmanuel?"

"I am from Nigeria."

"Really, so am I."

"Oh that's nice," and he turned back to the toilet. Sensing the conversation wouldn't go past that, I went into the living room and flipped on the Style network.

In less than ten minutes he came out of the bathroom and told me I shouldn't have any more problems with the toilet, but if I needed any help I could always call him. I thanked him and he left. I settled down to watch Fashion Police on Style. That Robert Verdi, he cracks me up. He had accosted some girl on the street and was querying her about her Fendi bag, was it real or fake. Of course she said real, but as she walked away he mouthed fake to the cameras. I laughed out loud.

As for Dele, naturally I had to call him and set up our date. So he's a little arrogant. At least he has the money to back it up. Some people are taxi drivers and are arrogant. Since he has admitted that he is attracted to me, why not oh jare? I called him and got his voice mail. I kept my message short and sweet: "Let's meet this Friday; you can pick me up at 8 pm."

Within minutes he texted me: "Friday won't work for me. How about Wednesday and you meet me at the supper club in Decatur."

"Fine," I texted back.

Now what was I going to wear? I went through my closet and saw nothing special enough. I looked at the time and it was 6 pm. I could just catch Saks at Phipps Plaza if I left right away.

I grabbed my purse and went to the elevator. As I was walking out the lobby, I noticed Emmanuel, but this time he was walking out also and looked very nice in dark jeans and a light sweater. He nodded and greeted me as I went by. I lifted up my hand in acknowledgment. As I pulled out of the parking lot in my 2000 Lexus Sedan, he was just getting into his car, a very old Toyota Tercel. I didn't even know they still made Tercels. Oh well, what a waste of muscles because I don't do broke, even if he is good looking!

Amaka

Fusion love

My plan was to out do myself in the kitchen for Jeffrey. I had planned this whole four course dinner -- it was going to be a fusion of Thai, African and French influences. Fortunately I had my friend Beverly over. She was a pharmacist like me, and so full of life. She is American but I have named her an honorary Nigerian. Beverly was in the kitchen with me while I was cooking, and gave me so much praise that I felt very confident in the meal. I was making a roast chicken in sweet and hot Thai sauce, Chinese style fried rice, shrimp and coconut milk infused moin-moin and slow cooked pulled lamb in a pastry shell with creamy mushroom sauce.

"This is so delish!" Beverly exclaimed while polishing off a piece of the chicken. I had roasted two: one for her and one for Jeffrey and me. She couldn't wait till she got home and so tore a drumstick as she sat at the breakfast bar in my kitchen and watched me assemble my dessert, mango cream with coconut flakes as a garnish.

Beverly is the kind of friend everyone needs, so full of energy, open to new experiences and fearless when it comes to adventure. There are so many Nigerians who live in America and do not have an American experience. I made an effort to: I have gone white water rafting, sailing, mountain hiking, even stayed on a Native American reservation. All this because I fully intended to enrich my life while in America, not just get the mighty dollar, and Beverly helped me reached that goal. We did it all together. We even went on a two week bike tour of Europe one summer because she signed us up. That summer was the fittest I have ever been.

Watching Beverly sitting there chewing on a chicken leg, I felt like she was my sister even though we were from totally different cultures and just met a couple of years ago. She had recently got married and just had a baby, and this was one of her few outings without the little one.

"Next time you come you have to bring little Damali with you. I haven't seen her since she was four months old!" I said while whipping my cream into submission.

"I know! She's so adorable now, crawling and getting into everything, my little Didi!"

"Your Didi, my little Ngozi, my blessing. I forgive you for not giving her a Nigerian name only because Damali is so beautiful. What does it mean again?"

"A beautiful vision in Swahili," Beverly explained. It was so Beverly to give her daughter a Swahili name, she was totally afrocentric. She had locks in her hair and everything; her husband had even renamed himself Kwame, dropping his given name Rodney. He was in politics, a state representative.

Beverly and Rodney, Kwame I mean, came from the same background. They were both fourth generation at Howard and had met there. They were part of the African American elite, the sort that know themselves as '*our kind of people*.' They are both alums of Jack and Jill, and Beverly is actually a Links member and Kwame a member of the Coalition of 100 Black Men. I remember going to one of their events and being condescended to until one of the men recognized my father who was an academic and a fairly well-known writer back home in Nigeria. If not for this, I would have continued to be an outsider, but instead, suddenly, I became a worthy sister from the continent.

Living in Atlanta allows you to meet more black professionals than you would typically come across, a group that is not only professional and moneyed, but also cultured. Some of them were extremely elitist and some even had an inferior view of Africa, but Beverly was not like that. She was informed and enlightened and took her family position and wealth as a privilege, not a right.

"So tell me more about this Jeffrey," Beverly said interrupting my thoughts.

"What's to tell? He is tall, sexy and romantic and I think I am falling for him," I said, pausing from my cooking.

"Really, that serious huh?"

"I think so, but you know me…the infatuation stage is so sweet."

"I know but something about this sounds different," Beverly said, half questioning.

"I hope so, we get on so well. He could really be the one!"

"Well, I hope so too." Beverly got up from the bar stool. She collected herself for a moment. Wiping her fingers on a napkin and smoothing out her cashmere sweater and lounge pant set, she came over and gave me a hug.

"Because you deserve it," she said, throwing her shawl over her shoulders. "Girl, I have got to run. Damali is probably driving Kwame crazy by now."

"Tell him I said hi, and I hope he enjoys the chicken."

"Oh I know he will," she said, patting her Tupperware container. "In fact, you know what, Maksy?"

"What?" I asked, looking at her.

"You should really consider becoming a caterer or a chef."

"You know something? I've been thinking about that more and more."

"Well, stop thinking and start doing."

"Someday I will," I said.

"Well, my dear, I have got to get going, because I have got to get somewhere and be somebody!" she said affecting the style of a Baptist preacher.

"You know it!"

Mina

Missing in Action

I changed my mind. Instead of making egusi, I decided to make edikaikong, vegetable stew. I would make it just the way he likes it too -- filled with orishirishi (assorted meats). The way I used to make it when we first started dating.

I laid out all of my ingredients: palm oil, dried and fresh shrimp, cow foot and skin, goat meat, a little chicken, even some periwinkles that I had managed to find at the Farmer's Market, and then spinach and ugu leaves. I started to cook and as I did, all the smells that I had previously kept out of my kitchen began to assault me. They took me back to my grandmother's kitchen, a place that was always warm and cozy and accepting. Everyone loved my grandmother, she was known for her warmth and generosity. She taught me how to cook. I missed her and sometimes, I wished I could be more like her.

The stew was ready, pretty good if I did say so myself. I only had a little taste. I couldn't eat traditional food if I wanted to keep my figure, so I had a bowl of salad with lemon juice for my dinner.

After that I made the pounded yam, it was piping hot and perfectly smooth. Then I set the table, using the Arte Italica china that I saved for special guests, and then I boiled some cinnamon sticks to get rid of the smell of the stew. When I was satisfied at how good it all looked, I went to the bathroom and got into a hot bath with Sake Bath gel. I always felt so sensual after bathing. I put on my favorite Felina bra and panty set, my kimono style caftan and my gold slippers. Then I went downstairs to wait for him.

I woke up with my neck hurting from sleeping in an awkward position on the couch. I looked over at the porcelain clock I had oohed and aahed over in Paris. Now its perfect shine seemed to mock me as it proclaimed: it is 2 am -- do you know where your husband is?

I got up to dial his cell phone. As I punched in the numbers I went over Obinna's call schedule in my head. He was not on call. Not tonight.

My call went directly to voicemail. Bells went off in my head: "What the hell is going on?"

I was contemplating my next move when I heard the key in the kitchen door. I just stood there by my beautifully set table and waited.

Obinna was humming to himself as he opened the door. When he saw me standing there he was startled. It took him a few seconds before he recovered to say, "Hello Mina, what are you doing up?"

"Waiting for you. I made dinner. I thought you weren't on call tonight."

"I wasn't. I had to cover for a friend."

"You could have called. I made you dinner," I said.

"I'm sorry. I didn't think it mattered. What did you make, salmon, chicken?"

"No, edikaikong," I spat out.

"Really?" Obinna asked, with his eyebrows raised. "Wow, I guess I can have it for lunch…" He trailed off, putting his things in his office.

"Like you are going to eat pounded yam in your lunch room."

"Why not? I'm still an African," he countered. "Anyway, I'm tired, I am going to bed." He walked over to me.

"Goodnight," he said, kissing me.

"Goodnight."

As he walked away towards the bedroom, all I could think about was the faint taste of egusi he left lingering on my lips.

I was clearing up my precious china when I heard a buzzing sound coming from Obinna's office. I placed the plates gingerly in the cabinet and then went to his office, brimming with curiosity. It sounded like his cell phone on vibrate. Who could be calling him at this hour?

Probably Nigeria, maybe some relative wanting money or something; they never called the house for some reason. I reached into his work bag and his blackberry indicated he had a text message. So I opened it.

I was shocked by the contents. It read: "My darling, just making sure u got home safe. Tonite was wonderful. C u tom. Love 4 ever."

I was floored.

So Obinna was cheating on me. Unbelievable! If someone had told me, I would never have believed it. So now the question is what to do? I stood up from the chair I had slumped into. I put his phone back into the bag and decided to go to sleep. I would think about this in the morning when I was more rational. Already so many rash thoughts had popped into my head, including slapping Obinna out of his sleep, the nerve of it. I was doing him a favor by being with him and he had the gall to cheat on me.

But even in my anger, as I looked around at my plush surroundings, I became painfully aware of my limited options. I had no money of my own, no job and no experience. Even if I could get a great divorce settlement, my lifestyle would change drastically. I had to sleep on it, to think about what I really wanted. I slipped into the sheets next to Obinna who was already snoring softly. As I looked at him sprawled out on his side of our California king, I knew I wasn't going to leave him. I made him what he was and I would be damned if some egusi-cooking bitch would snatch it away.

Titi

The supper club

I had never been to this place. It was very romantic, very boudoir chic. I have to admit, Dele was looking so good in his charcoal suit and light gray shirt. I was so glad that I had invested four hundred plus into this Nicole Miller number. The halter top put my cleavage on full and sexy display, and the skirt hinted at the roundness of my hips.

As soon as I got close enough to say hello, he pulled me in for a kiss. I was a little taken aback but I went along with it. He was a great kisser and soon I started to get lost in his embrace. As soon as I started to swoon, he released me.

"Let's get something to eat," he said hoarsely.

"Okay." We followed the waitress to our table.

"We'll have a bottle of the Chateau Croix de Labrie, and the lady will have hand-stuffed ravioli with fresh mozz, roasted tomato with thyme tomato butter, and I'll have Australian organic filet mignon on black pepper grits."

"You ordered for me, how do you know if I'll even like the ravioli?" I queried, appalled at his bad manners.

"Trust me, you will." He was so smug. His arrogance was getting less bearable.

"You look very sexy tonight," Dele said smiling.

I forgave him slightly.

"Is that all your hair?" he asked.

"Excuse me?" I was shocked; it was so rude of him to ask.

"It doesn't really matter to me, I just like to know for future reference," Dele said pointedly.

What kind of future reference, stupid man, if not that he had so much potential, I for no dey take this nonsense.

"Yes it is." Okay, so I lied. It isn't his business anyway.

"Good." He leaned back into his seat and stared at me intently.

"Excuse me?" I said.

"You are prettier than I expected," he said.

"You're more of a jerk than I expected," I countered.

He laughed. "Touché, I'm sorry. I guess I'm so used to dealing tough in the corporate world, I sometimes forget to take my suit off, so to speak." Dele smiled apologetically.

I began to think that there might be hope for this night after all so I conceded gracefully: "It's okay, we all have our issues."

"So tell me about yourself... Why isn't a beautiful woman like you married with a boatload of children yet?"

"Well, I don't know about the boatload of children but I guess I haven't met the right guy as far as marriage is concerned."

"Ok, what's your idea of the right guy?" he probed.

"Oh you know, God fearing, intelligent, good heart all that…" I gave a trite response.

"You didn't say rich and handsome," he said smiling.

"Well, handsome is relative and of course I want my man to be successful but money doesn't have to define him." I was blowing grammar. I am not crazy. I can't really tell him that the fellow better have cash and be solidly fine, after all, who wants to suffer?

"Interesting, I would have thought you would be looking for something different," he said.

"Like what?" I raised my eyebrows in interest.

"Can I be honest?" he asked.

"Of course," I said sweetly.

"It's just that most of our girls tend to be very materialistic," he stated, while swirling the wine around in his glass.

"Well, I guess, it's a byproduct of our society," I said, trying to look thoughtful.

"Indeed." He sniffed the wine.

"So why haven't *you* settled down yet?" I asked him.

"I guess like you I'm looking for the right woman," he smiled, finally taking a sip.

"And she would be?" I inquired.

"Oh you know, God fearing, intelligent, good heart…all that," he smiled naughtily.

I laughed and he joined me.

Then the waiter brought our meal. The ravioli was delicious and the wine was exquisite and Mr. Dele Thompson, well I could just eat him up.

Amaka

African Orchids

When I opened the door for Jeffrey, I was struck again by how attracted I was to him. He smiled and I melted. He was carrying a ceramic pot of beautiful orchids.

"I was in the flower shop and they were trying to give me roses but when I saw these orchids I knew they were the right flowers to get. They reminded me of you -- beautiful, intense and exotic."

Never before had I been described in those terms. I took the pot from him and placed it on my coffee table and kissed him in response. When my lips touched his, he put his arms around me and gently drew me to his chest. It was a passionate kiss, but it was also slow and languid. We stood there for a while, exploring and luxuriating in each other and then my oven timer went off.

I leaned back and looked at him. He smiled at me and caressed my back.

"I guess we have to stop for dinner," he said, "although I'd rather go straight to dessert." He held me away from me and looked at me intently, as if trying to take me in.

"I have made a serious meal and so we are going to eat," I said walking away from him towards the kitchen. I was wearing a simple floor length matte jersey caftan that clung to my every curve and I was barefoot but my toes were polished beautifully by Mei Ling at the nail shop I frequented.

As I walked towards the dining room I noticed he wasn't following me. "Aren't you coming?"

"In a minute. Right now, I would like to enjoy the view," he said.

I smiled as I turned away and walked with an extra sway in my walk. I was enjoying him enjoying me.

We had finished our dinner and we were having dessert in bed. Actually we were each other's dessert, and the mango cream was just an extra. He leaned into me and kissed me with the cream on his tongue. It was sweet and exhilarating. This was a man who I had completely fallen in love with.

He put a little of the cream on my shoulder and then he kissed it off, then a little on my neck and he kissed it off too. Then he placed a little on my chest right at the top of my cleavage. When he kissed me there, he eased my dress down over my shoulders and soon it dropped to the floor. I started to reach for the cover and he pulled it gently away from me saying, "Leave it, I want to see you."

I was excited and nervous at the same time. I thought about my body. I alternated between loving and hating it. I loved my curves and how they made me feel sexy, but I also hated them when I thought about svelte bodies like Halle Berry's without an ounce of fat. My stomach was a little rounded and my hips were definitely full and the cups of my demi-bra were literally running over. Jeffrey exhaled.

"You are so beautiful." He caressed my arms and looked at me while shaking his head. "You are so beautiful in every way and I can't believe you are mine." I was so moved by his words. We kissed again and then we fell onto my bed.

For the millionth time I was pleased that I had splurged on my bed. It was quite expensive, almost twice my budget, but I had laid on it and knew I had to have it. It was truly heavenly, just soft enough. And my Bellino 500 thread count linens may have cost me quite some money but every time I lay in my bed, I knew they were worth it. That night as we both lay there naked, I felt I could stay like that forever.

I woke up to the sounds of pages rustling. Jeffrey was sitting up in bed, reading a book. I looked closer and I saw it was my favorite book of poetry, Ruth Forman's *Renaissance*.

"Are you enjoying it?" I asked.

He looked over at me. "You are awake."

"Yes," I said, yawning softly. I snuggled closer; I liked waking up next to him.

"I didn't know you liked poetry…you are truly a renaissance woman." He leaned over to kiss me.

"You think so?" I said, smiling.

"Yes, how many women can be as beautiful, cook so well, be so intellectual and so damn sexy all at the same time?" He continued, "I have truly found a gem."

Mina

Investigative Reporting

I hated to be a snoop, but I had to know what I was dealing with here. Ever since I found out my Obinna was cheating on me, I had become obsessed with getting more information, and since there is no way I would hire a private detective, lest someone find out, I planned to do all the digging myself.

So far, I had found quite a bit of information. Apparently Obinna must have thought I would never know about the affair because he didn't cover his tracks very well.

First stop was his computer. He spends endless hours in his office on his computer and I always assumed he was doing something harmless like playing chess. However what I found was mind boggling. Obinna, who I had previously thought was so pedestrian as far as sex was concerned, had a healthy collection of online porn. It was hidden in a file called medical jargon. It was jargon alright!

Now the porn itself wasn't necessarily the kicker. What was amazing was that the women were all quite -- well there's no good way to put it -- they were fat! Not horrendously so, just a little extra meat on their bones that settled mostly in their boobs and butts. I looked at my B cups which I was ordinarily very proud of, and suddenly they looked so small and uninviting. These women were working with some serious assets. My goodness! They looked more like Amaka than they did me. Come to think of it, I remember times when Obinna seemed to be giving Amaka an appreciative once over, his eyes lingering just a little too long.

I was floored. I thought he was attracted to petite women like me, though of course I had been slightly fleshier in college. As I was contemplating his shift in taste, I stumbled across his collection of her love letters or emails, I should say.

"Obinna, I want to thank you so much for everything. You have made me so happy. I am so blessed to have you in my life."

What does she mean blessed? Blessed with another woman's husband! I don't know why people always call God's name when God has nothing to do with it.

"Obi sweetie, I can't wait for our trip to North Carolina. I have been waiting all week, and in fact I have planned something special for our first night there."

North Carolina! The bastard! No wonder he refused to take me with him, he took her! And what hurts me the most is that I was ovulating then.

"Obi my love, thank you so much for the car. You don't know what you have done for me. I love you so much and I can't wait till we can really be together."

Oh hell no! Did she say he bought her a car, when for a good year I have been telling him to upgrade my Mercedes SUV!

I couldn't believe him. I was totally undone. The ungrateful wretch, after everything I had done for him. I tell you no good deed goes unpunished.

I was so shocked that momentarily I didn't know what to do. Then my eyes were drawn to a glinting on my finger. I looked down and saw it was the diamond on my finger picking up the rays of the sun. A three carat brilliant cut, internally flawless diamond set in platinum. I still remember the day we went to Tiffany's and picked it out. Well, I picked it out while Obinna just stood there trying to get over his sticker shock. Thinking now about that day, I remembered what I had to do: I had to fight for my marriage; I had to protect my way of life.

I decided to check the reverse phone directory and get her name. I punched in her number and there it was: Carolina Okafor. Carolina? What kind of classless name was Carolina? I couldn't believe that Obinna was cheating on me with someone called Carolina. The number hung there on the screen daring me to do what I really wanted to. Call the woman and curse her out, but I couldn't do that. First off it would not be ladylike and secondly, it could definitely backfire, especially since from her letters it looked like they were having a pretty serious relationship. The question now was how to win my husband back and get her out of the picture.

I didn't know how to start. I wished I could talk to Amaka or even Titi about this but I couldn't let them know that all wasn't well for me. What would they think? What would everyone think, that Mina Duru has been one-upped, and by a Carolina no less.

I was going crazy. I had to tell someone. Since I couldn't tell my Naija girls, I had to tell the only other person I could confide in. My friend, Chanterelle!

Chanterelle was my only close American friend. We met when I first moved to the States and had remained close ever since. She was my "I got your back" friend. Titi and Maksy had my back to an extent but Chanterelle was ready to go above and beyond. I didn't hang with Chanterelle too much because in spite of her high heels and professional suit, she always managed to get into one altercation or another. I mean once we went out to a club and she almost got into it with some girl who stepped on her shoes. Well, as Chanterelle put it, they were Jimmy Choos!

Now don't think Chanterelle is some kind of ghetto bunny. She is a professional sister, a PR exec in one of the top firms in Atlanta. She is just hot-tempered and a little excitable.

Anyway, I knew Chanterelle would know what to do, or at least she would make me feel better about the whole situation. So I called her.

"Hey girl," she said when she answered.

"Hey yourself, how are you?"

"Oh you know, another day, another dollar," she sighed.

I went straight to the point and told her what was going on. She listened intently, occasionally peppering the conversation with shouts of "Oh hell no!" and "What!" When I finished, she sighed again and asked me, "So what do you want to do?"

"Honestly," I replied, "I wish I could beat them both up."

"O.K! You know I got your back!"

My girl! I told you she always had my back. Chanterelle was so bad that I could see her taking her dainty foot out of her Jimmy Choos and really kicking someone's ass.

"However on a serious note, it sounds like you really need to assess your situation and decide what it is you really want."

"What do you mean what I want? Obviously I want my husband!" I said with more than a trace of irritation.

"Are you sure?" she prodded. "Sounds like you're more into the lifestyle than him."

"Whatever," I said.

"Look Mina, I don't mean to piss you off, but you have to hear the truth."

"Which is…?"

"Which is that you never really loved Obinna, so maybe this is life's way of forcing you to deal with that."

"Chanterelle, I called you for advice on how to deal with this bitch who is stealing my husband, and you are telling me this?"

"Well, ok I'm sorry. What would you like me to say?"

"I'd like you to come with me to confront the girl."

"I don't think that's wise," she said. "Your beef is not with her, but with your husband."

"Look, I thought you said you had my back?"

"I do, Mina, but all that fighting and crazy stuff was fine when we were kids but we're grown now and that should change."

"You know what, Chanterelle? I think I'll handle this on my own."

"Fine, suit yourself," she said, "but really I hope you will consider…"

"Click." I hung up the phone in her ear. After all the nonsense I followed her to do when she needed me, now she wants to preach to me about love. Who needs her!

Amaka

Caught up in the rapture

Could things get any sweeter than this? Jeffrey and I were enjoying a lazy afternoon watching football on TV when he started tracing something on my back.

"What are you doing?" I asked while arching my back in pleasure.

"Making my mark," he explained. "Actually I am writing something."

"What?" I asked again.

"Something I never expected to be writing," he said grinning.

"Stop teasing me and tell me," I demanded.

"I am writing…," he paused, "I love you."

I was silent and I could feel the blood rushing to my head. Did he just say he loved me? Why? I never asked or pressured him. I never told him that I loved him even though I have felt that for some time. If he is saying it with no pressure then it must be true. After all, if it was just about sex, well he has already had that.

"Why are you quiet? Did I upset you?" Jeffrey asked softly.

"Of course not," I said. "I guess I didn't expect to feel this way either. I love you too."

He smiled and then leaned in for a kiss. I met his lips with fervor.

If there was a definition of hot and steamy, it was us. It was truly a whirlwind romance. Just when I started to feel like things couldn't get any better, the dreams started.

First it was just strange little things like I'd dream that we would be eating and he would try and feed me a piece of chocolate and then when I looked down it would be an onion. Then the dreams became more overt. I would dream about him leaving the house and a woman holding a baby waving as he left. I always dream when something is not right and in my heart I knew something was not right.

I also started noticing that he would never call Nigeria in my presence and when I spent the night, occasionally Jeffrey would answer the phone in hushed, whispered tones. Initially I thought nothing of it, but combined with the dreams and the fact that I thought I heard him say sweetheart on the phone one day, I had to confront him with my concerns.

At first he hedged the questions and played down my concerns but as I continued to press him he eventually admitted that there was something he hadn't told me. I held my breath as Jeffrey spoke:

"I'm sorry, I should have told you right from the beginning, but I felt you wouldn't want anything to do with me."

My heart began to pound in my chest. What was he going to say? Would this mean the end of the relationship? Was he really too good to be true?

"I have a child. She is six. I am no longer with the mother but there it is," Jeffrey blurted out.

I was torn between irritation and relief. A child I could deal with, it was better than the alternative, but I was a little upset that he didn't tell me before. I had a right to know before I got involved and I told him so. He apologized and looked so dejected.

"I guess now I'm going to lose you?"

I was quiet. I didn't quite know what to say.

He came close and put his arms on my shoulders. "I love you. I wish that I had met you before but I love my daughter and she will always be part of my life."

I remained quiet. The fantasy I had created was not quite gelling. I always wanted for my husband and me to share the first childbirth together. Now my child would always be second in his mind, if we even went that far.

"Baby, please don't shut me out because of this. I should have told you I know, but it doesn't change how I feel about you."

I looked at him. He was so handsome and looked so sincere and I was already so deeply in love with him, how could I walk away? What if he was my soul mate? My one true love? Surely passion like ours doesn't come around twice?

I decided to throw caution to the wind. This was the kind of love I had been waiting for all my life; I was not going to let it go over a technicality. I would be a great stepmother if it came to that, but her mother was a different story.

"What's the deal with her mother?" I asked.

"Well, honestly I just dated her in passing and I guess she was so determined to be Mrs. Jeffrey Ifedike that she got pregnant."

"What do you mean, she got pregnant? She didn't do it alone," I said with slight annoyance. "I mean you could have used a condom."

"I should have, but she told me she was on the pill."

"So you two are no longer together?"

"No, I broke up with her and then she told me she was pregnant. She tried to pressure me into marrying her and honestly, initially, I tried. She moved in with me and my father started proceedings for a traditional marriage but I couldn't stand it and I pulled out very quickly."

I didn't know how to feel. My Prince Charming was losing some of his sparkle.

"I am not proud of the whole situation but it is what it is. My parents are still sore on the topic because as good Igbo parents they expected me to do the right thing." He continued: "I love my child definitely, but sometimes, especially like in a situation like this, I wish the whole thing had never happened." He looked at me pleadingly.

I looked at him and while I just wanted to fall into his arms and say it was alright, that I loved him anyway, my mind kept screaming caution, caution.

He continued speaking, "I know that I haven't known you very long but you are the one I have been searching for. I honestly had started to doubt I could feel this way about anyone. You make me feel alive. I can't even explain it. Since I met you, I think about you constantly and sometimes just recalling something you said or the way you looked at a certain moment makes me smile, and I truly want to be with you always. You are different from any other woman I know. The conversations we have and the way we connect emotionally and physically just blow me away." He reached for me, put his hands around my waist and pulled me close. He bent his head to my ear.

"I love you. Don't leave me."

My mind was racing through so many different scenarios, but in my heart all I wanted to do was sink deep onto his chest and feel his heart beat against mine.

I chose to believe him.

When he moved to kiss me, I parted my lips and put my arms around him.

He sighed with pleasure.

Titi

Spring Cleaning

My new furniture had just come in. It was a beautiful chocolate velvet sofa and a pink and sage chaise with brown detailing. I was sitting in my living room admiring how it looked especially against my mocha walls and hardwood floors. I was also looking at my new draperies that I had made. They were chocolate silk with green panels.

I got out my step stool and started hanging my curtains when the stool slipped and I ended up falling heavily onto the floor. I hit my butt pretty hard and so I was still sitting there when I heard a knock on the door.

"Are you alright?" the voice queried.

I recognized it but I couldn't quite place it.

"Yes, I'm fine. Who are you?"

"It's Emmanuel. Do you need some help?"

Since I could actually use his help, I said a resounding yes. I told him to wait while I opened the door. However when I tried to stand to my feet, the pain in my tail bone was so sharp that I cried out.

"Ok, don't move; I have a master key which is only to be used during emergencies. If you want I can open the door and come and help you."

I started to think about it. Was it wise to let him come in? What if he meant me harm? But if so he wouldn't have asked, he would have come in already. I looked around for a heavy object. There was a bronze sculpture that I got in Accra. If he tried anything, I could knock him over the head with it. I made sure that it was within easy reach and then I said, "Okay."

I heard the key turning in the lock.

"Are you alright?" Emmanuel asked again.

"I seem to have hurt myself a little."

"Can you stand up?" He crouched down to offer help. I tried but the pain was so intense that I cried out again.

"Okay," he said, resolved. "I will have to carry you."

"Carry me where?"

"Well, it appears that you may have hit your coccyx and that's what is causing the pain. It is probably a little sore," he said.

"What do you mean my coccyx?" I asked. I had no idea what a coccyx was.

"I mean your tailbone."

"Oh," I said.

"I am going to place you in your bed and then run a bath for you with some Epsom salts, that and some Ibuprofen should help."

Emmanuel placed me on my bed and then went to run my bath water. I heard him puttering about in there and humming to himself and then he knocked on my door.

"Your bath is ready, and if you like I can put you in it."

I had just taken some Ibuprofen and decided to let him help me. He picked me up fully dressed and then placed me on a stool by the bath.

"Just undress and when you are ready use your arms to lift yourself into the bath," he suggested, demonstrating.

"Okay," I said. "Thanks."

"No problem and later I can help you with your curtains." He was getting ready to leave when the door was flung open by Segun.

Emmanuel looked ready to swing.

Segun looked ready to kill.

"What the hell are you doing here with my girl?" Segun demanded

I started to protest: "Segun, it's not what you think."

"You shut up, bitch!" he snapped.

"Look, I am the building manager and I was simply helping her. She just had a nasty fall."

Segun looked at me and I tried to have my most mournful look on my face.

"It's true," I said. "Emmanuel, thanks but I think you better leave. Thanks again."

As soon as Emmanuel left, Segun reached back and slapped me.

"So you want to make a fool of me, eh?"

"Segun, stop it," I used my hands to shield myself. "I'm telling the truth! I hurt myself. I fell. There is nothing going on between myself and this man."

"Do you think he can give you what I give you?"

"Segun, I have already told you there is nothing going on between us; I mean he is a maintenance man for goodness sake."

That seemed to calm him down. For a man as insanely arrogant and vain as Segun, the idea of a woman leaving him for a common handyman was unfathomable.

But the whole episode showed me just how vulnerable I was. I had let this go on for far too long. Yes, there was a time that I felt I had no choice but to tolerate Segun's craziness, but over time he has gotten more and more violent and I'm not so stupid that I can't see the danger. The problem is that I don't think the typical things like restraining orders and such will make a difference in this matter. I just have to think carefully about what to do.

Amaka

Undesirable elements

"So he is married basically?"

Titi was working my nerves! Ever since I told her about Jeffrey, she had been insisting that his story was not complete.

"Something doesn't add up," she kept saying.

I couldn't understand her, his story made total sense to me. I mean what's so unbelievable about a guy making a mistake and having a child out of wedlock. I know so many guys with babies by various African-American women out here and most of them didn't get married, they just have baby mama drama.

"Titi, for the last time, he never married her. They just have a child together."

"So he says," she insisted. "Either way na too much wahala!" Titi shook her head. "I know you feel like this Jeffrey is the best thing since sliced bread, but I don't want you to get hurt here."

"I am not going to," I said determinedly. "He loves me."

"Okay O, don't say I didn't warn you."

Just then this fine waiter came to pour some water for us both and brought some bread.

"Are you ladies ready to order?"

"Definitely," Titi said. "For some reason, I'm ravenous.

"I'll have the Chinese chicken salad." I loved the salads at California Pizza Kitchen, they were so delish!

"And I've have the garlic chicken pizza with shrimp added," Titi said.

"Okay, will that be all?" the waiter asked.

"Yes, thank you," we both said in unison. No one can say we Naija babes don't have manners.

"So how was your date with the wonderful Mr. Thompson?"

"Well, it started out kind of rocky but by the end of the night, it was great," Titi said, smiling.

"Oh really, so did you …?" I asked knowingly.

"Did I what? Reach the heights of pleasure and rock his world?" she said laughing. "No, I am saving that for a later date!"

"What! You are waiting!?" I exclaimed. "Stop the presses, this is serious."

"Shut up, Maksy, someone hearing you will think I'm a slut. For your information, I do not sleep with every man I meet." Titi feigned irritation. "Just the ones with big shekinis," she added breaking into a wide smile.

"Titi! Don't be so crass." I was embarrassed because the old white ladies at the table next to us had started to peer at us with disapproval.

"Whatever oh jare, I don't know why everyone acts like sex is such a big deal. You all do it. Even these ladies eavesdropping on our conversation do it, and it's all good," Titi said, turning to stare pointedly at the ladies.

They turned red in embarrassment and promptly asked their waiter if they could change tables. As we watched them shuffle off, Titi made an announcement.

"I think he may be the one."

"Who? What one?" I asked, feeling a little clueless.

"Dele, you idiot, he might be the one."

"What, but you have just had one date!" I said, shocked. Usually Titi was so practical. It wasn't like her to get carried away.

She looked so earnest as she explained: "I know, I know, it's just that I can feel something different here. I think he really gets me. I feel like maybe I can be myself with him."

"Are you sure? Maybe you should take it slow?"

"Oh I plan to; you know you can't rush perfection."

That being said I decided to move on to a more sensible topic.

"So what do you think is going on with Mina?" I asked. "I tried calling her a couple of times last week, but she never even called back."

"I guess maybe she is still upset that I called her frigid," Titi shrugged.

"You were pretty harsh," I volunteered.

Titi looked outraged. "Me! The woman practically called me a whore."

"You know you have a tougher skin than Mina," I replied.

"Oh, so that gives you all license to just abuse me?" she said, looking very hurt.

"Titi, I didn't say that. I'm just worried about Mina."

"Sorry, jo…I guess she hurt my feelings, even though I didn't show it. Anyway I think she and Obinna are going through something."

"Something like what?"

"You know, something. Maybe they are having trouble conceiving," Titi mulled it over.

"She never said she wanted a child. I thought she wanted to be one of those DINK families," I said.

"What is dink?"

"You know, dual income no kids," I explained. "It's a marketing term."

"But Mina doesn't have an income."

"Obinna's income is like two incomes," I offered.

"I heard that! That's what I'm talking about!"

I tried to remain serious. "So why do you think she is having trouble?"

"Mina is the quintessential Naija babe, always acting like everything is perfect, meanwhile yawa don blow for house," Titi sermonized.

"But to be infertile?" I said. "Mina is just modern; she doesn't necessarily want a whole bunch of kids running around. Imagine kids in that beautiful house of hers, so much to break and scatter," I said.

"Ehen, if she is modern, is her mother-in-law modern too? You think the first son of an Igbo isn't under pressure to have children? You think she is happy that some Rivers girl came and took her son and to top it all, won't give her a grandchild? Why are you acting like you don't know your people?"

"Well, you do have a point," I conceded.

"Of course, I know what I am talking about." Titi continued, "Anyway sha O, my own is that if she doesn't want to talk about it, me I won't bring it up. That is why I was telling her to loosen up, if she can't have a baby, then she better bring something else to the table. She better shake bodi and stop acting like some damn princess all the time."

"Gosh, poor Mina."

"Poor Mina what? I beg, she is not the first and she will not be the last. All I am saying she better get herself together before her mother-in-law brings some Ngozi to come and take her husband," Titi said, before taking a bite of her pizza.

"Why does it have to be an Ngozi now," I said laughing.

"You know you Igbo girls, it's always an Ngozi!"

Mina

Fast chick factor

I can't believe I didn't see this coming. I found out who the Carolina person was. She is one of the nursing assistants in Obinna's hospital.

Can you imagine! A nursing assistant, not even a nurse! I even hear the girl is fresh off the boat from Naija and not even of our class at home either. She used to sell bread in the market. My husband wants to be with a bread seller over me! Can you just imagine the nonsense!

Foolish man, the girl is probably one of these fast chicks determined to better her way in life by any means necessary. So she wants to destroy my home to do it. Stupid bitch, I will show her P for pepper! Nonsense! And as for Obinna, after everything I have done for him, this is how he repays me. The bastard, if he is not careful, I will divorce him and take him for everything he owns, after all he is the one that is cheating!

Just goes to show you how the good are truly undervalued in this world. I take this classless man and make him into something worthwhile and then I give him the ultimate gift, me: a beautiful, sought after woman with class and sophistication. But in the end he still goes back to lie in the trash. I guess a dog is a dog no matter what -- you can bathe him, groom him, even dress him up with a nice collar, but first chance he gets, he'll run off and stick his nose in some shit.

Honestly, I can't believe this. This is really some shit!

Yes, I know I swore and that is unbecoming of a lady but this situation demands it. SHIT, SHIT, SHIT!!!

I wish I could tell Amaka and Titi, because this is all swirling around in my brain and I feel like I am going to explode, but if I tell them, who knows they might go laughing behind my back about how the mighty have fallen. Tonight is our girls' night. I decided to have it as planned because until I know how I am going to proceed with this, I don't want anyone to know what's going on.

Amaka

Great Expectations

Sometimes I feel like a piece of coal trapped under a world of pressure, except I wonder if I'll turn into a diamond or simply be crushed under the weight of it. My mother is trying to drive me crazy! Every day she calls me or flashes me from Nigeria.

Flashing is when she lets it ring long enough for it to register on your caller ID but not long enough for you to actually pick up the call. When she flashes, I am supposed to call her back immediately. If I don't, she has been known to flash repeatedly. The other day she flashed me almost ten times in an hour; I had my cell phone on vibrate and by the end of the meeting I was stuck in, I felt like I was at the nail salon in the vibrating chair.

When I finally called her back, she picked up on the first ring.

"I've been flashing you." Her manner was accusing.

"I know, Mummy, I was in a meeting," I said quietly, trying to stop myself from screaming at her.

"Oh, you were at work, I thought you were off today?" It's funny, my mother lives thousands of miles away from me, yet she still tries to monitor my movements.

"Yes, it's my day off, but I had a continuing education class to attend."

"Okay, no problem," she said.

And then there was silence. Mind you I am paying per minute for this phone call to Nigeria and she is taking the time to be silent.

"Is everything alright, Mummy?" I asked.

"Yes O," she said and then she let out a long sigh.

I held my tongue, obviously something was on her mind, and from past experience I knew that pushing her would be ineffective. I decided to go the idle chit chat route.

"So how is business?" I enquired.

"Terrible, but God dey." The standard Nigerian response. "The market is not moving like before and the jewelry that I have sold, well these women don't want to pay, not to mention that we have no light, and diesel for the generator is so expensive! Anyway, it is well." Another standard platitude.

"Amen O, Mummy," I said, somewhat desensitized to her plight.

"Anyway, you know who I ran into at Shoprite this morning?"

How could I possibly know? Nigeria is the most populous country in Africa, it could have been anyone. I remained silent.

"Ah, you don't want to guess, ok let me tell you; it was Nneka, you know Aunty Nkiru's daughter who was two years below you in school. Can you imagine she has been married for four years and has three boys and one more on the way. Amaka, she looked so happy and I understand that her husband does well for himself as well. She asked of you. I told her you were doing well, but still unmarried and she said she thought she might know some eligible men. Isn't that exciting?" she gushed. She had spewed all this out in a rush, barely stopping to take a breath.

The girl she was referring to was a couple of years behind me at school and she was a snot-nosed brat then and I heard that she is even snottier now.

"Shall I give her your number, so you two can connect?" she asked.

"No," I responded very quickly. The last thing I needed was some arrogant brat feeling sorry for me.

"Well, then let me give you hers; please make sure you call her, because you know time is not on your side."

I wanted to tell her about Jeffrey so badly. I wanted her to see the kind of man I actually had. I wanted to laugh in perfect Mrs. Nneka's face and shout: "He who laughs last, laughs best," but I knew I couldn't. There were too many loose ends that needed to be tied up first.

For a moment I allowed myself to daydream about a wedding. We would get married in Atlanta, of course, at the Biltmore Ballrooms. I had attended a wedding there once and I immediately fell in love with the place. However I also loved the Atlanta Botanical Gardens; that would work if it was a fall wedding. I knew that I was going to wear a Reem Acra gown. I loved the way she cut for real women's curves and her ornate embroidery. It would be a beautiful wedding.

My mother's voice pulled me back into reality. "Amaka, you have to stop being so picky. Just settle down with a man and believe me, this love that you are looking for will come."

If only she knew that I had found it already.

Titi

No condition is permanent

I decided to reward Emmanuel for his help. He had actually come and hung my curtains and fixed my garbage disposal. Each time he came he was so quiet, but I found that I still enjoyed his company. So I decided to make him dinner. Okay, fine I decided to order dinner.

There is this restaurant, Queens, in Atlanta and the chef there makes a pretty good edikaikong, but naturally as with all things Naija, you can't expect your order to be produced in a timely fashion, so I called almost two hours before I was ready to pick up. On my way out of the restaurant, what did I hear but "Hey baby, can I talk to you" in a very thick Lagos accent. I turned around and the fellow looked totally like an area boy—read street thug—with his extra baggy jeans and his wife beaters. I guess the fact that he was leaning against his S class was supposed to sway me.

"I'm sorry, I have somewhere I need to be," I responded as I opened my car and got in, in the words of one of my favorite characters from the movies, "As if!" I am not so desperate that I will date potential drug dealers or 419 boys; after all, I am still trying to figure out how to get rid of Segun.

Emmanuel came over in the evening with his tool box. When I told him that I didn't have anything to fix, but just wanted to thank him with a little dinner, he looked really uncomfortable. It took a lot of reassurance before he would agree to sit down and eat with me. He was virtually silent as usual. He refused wine or beer and drank only water, but did take a large helping of the pounded yam and edikaikong, occasionally sighing with pleasure. I had the sense that it had been a while since he had had home cooking.

"Are you enjoying the food?" I asked.

"Very much," he admitted. "My mother used to cook me vegetable stew like this.

"You cook very well." Emmanuel smiled at me with gratitude. I opened my mouth to tell him I hadn't cooked it, and then I shut it again. I guess part of me wanted to enjoy the illusion.

I started to talk about Nigerian food I missed; authentic street food like bole and roasted groundnut. He talked about eko and moi-moi, and before you know it we were reminiscing about growing up in Nigeria and smacking our lips thinking about the local delicacies.

By the end of the evening we were laughing and relaxed. He stood up to leave at around ten and I found myself not wanting him to go. He felt like a brother to me. It's funny I have about 15 half brothers and sisters and I don't know any of them. I guess that's why I felt so close to Emmanuel. He reminded me of the family I had always longed for.

Amaka

Romping in Rio

Jeffrey surprised me with a trip to Brazil. When he asked me to clear my schedule, I was a little hesitant until he showed me the tickets he had purchased. It took a little cajoling but I got one of my colleagues to cover for me, so I had about five days off.

It had been a little weird between us ever since I found out about his child. He had been trying hard to make it right, but somehow, the tension was still there. I wanted to move on but I just couldn't go back to how it was. We still went out and we still were together in every sense of the word, but there was a level of connection that was lost.

Jeffrey sensed it and tried everything to prove to me that he was sincerely in love with me. He told me everyday, sent flowers, cooked, cleaned, waxed lyrical in the bedroom. I mean it was serious and I really did love him. I had totally fallen for everything about him, but

Titi's words kept coming back to haunt me: *What if he's married?*

I didn't believe that he was, how could any man be married and still be so passionate with me? I never pressed him to tell me his feelings. I never asked him where we were going or what his intentions were towards me. I just took each day as it came. It was him that kept professing his love and this was after he had chewed, knacked, totally hit it—however you want to put it—so presumably it wasn't just about sex. He already had that so why would he go further and talk about love, except that he meant it?

So when he begged me to go to Sao Paulo with him, because he had a conference to attend there, even though I said no initially, I knew that I would eventually go.

The trip was wonderful. It started with a first class non-stop trip from Atlanta to Sao Paulo; then we relaxed at the lovely Hilton Sao Paulo Morumbi. As soon as we walked into the lobby, I knew we would be happy there. It was done up in a very modern way and was very appealing. The décor in the room was consistent and we liked it. It helped that we were given complementary chocolates and champagne in the room.

We were a bit tired from the trip, but still found the energy to go down to the bar and have a couple of caprihinias, Brazil's national drink.

The rest of the trip went by in a blur. Jeffrey went to his conference during the day and I spent the day shopping or swimming or generally hanging around. At night we would go out to dinner or go dancing at a club close by. We were only there for four days and before I knew it we were on the plane back to Atlanta.

On the flight back, I nestled my head into Jeffrey's shoulder, feeling very content and happy. He reached down to pull a strand of hair out of my face. I noticed his Ebel watch glinted in the light. Well, I thought it was his watch then I realized it wasn't a watch at all -- it was a diamond ring!

I sat up and looked at him. He held the ring in his hand. It was an engagement ring. He started to speak and I saw his mouth move but I didn't hear the words; I was momentarily stunned by what was happening. Heck, I had no idea what was happening. I chastised myself for not paying attention and tuned back in.

He was saying how much he loved me and how I had showed him what it was like to really be alive. He started talking about how even though it had only been a couple of months he was sure he wanted to spend the rest of his life with me.

But he was asking me to accept the ring as a promise to be engaged. He told me that he had some things he had to sort out, not least of which was his child. Once he sorted them out, he would officially propose and talk to my parents, but until that time he asked me to keep everything under wraps as he didn't want a situation where his child's mother made things difficult.

He wanted me to erase any doubts I had about him in my head. He said again that he didn't want to lose me.

I looked at him, this handsome, charming man and thought about the conversations we had had. How good his arms felt around me. How he made me feel when he kissed my collarbone. How he rubbed my feet.

I thought to myself: this must be what love is.

I accepted the ring. He put it on my finger and suddenly I saw a kaleidoscope of colors as the diamonds caught the light.

Titi

Looking for Mrs. Thompson

Dele Thompson had been steadily rocking my world. What's that Janet Jackson song "Anytime, Anyplace..."? Anyway that was our level.

Even though things were piping hot between us, being with Dele took some getting used to. Things had to be his way or the highway. There was no middle ground. We met on his terms, whenever it was convenient for him.

However when we first got together there was one thing that I thought I couldn't get past. It wasn't his arrogance because after a while, I got used to that. Neither was it his domineering manner: the fact that he orders for me, makes demands and tries to tell me what to do. No, those things I could handle, they tend to come in the Naija betta boy package. It was his freakiness that I was thrown by.

When you see Dele Thompson, you picture him as a straight-laced fellow, with his monogrammed shirts and bespoke suits. But underneath all that fine linen lay a man and a freak.

The man likes piercings.

He has both of his nipples pierced. That was a bit unexpected but fine, I was a little turned on by it. However, as I began to work my way down, I was shocked to see that he had one more piercing and you'll never guess where! Well, I gave it away already abi? Can you imagine, he had his shekini, the man had his penis pierced! Of all the freaky mcnasties…!

I guess he saw my look of shock and felt he had to say something.

"Don't worry, you will love this! I got it in Amsterdam and trust me it will make you feel so good."

I looked at him and I have to admit, in spite of my shock, I started to get somewhat hot. I mean this guy was built like a Greek god. Ripples in all the right places and after checking out his solid eight plus inches, the ring at the end started to look less like an instrument of torture and more like the icing on the cake.

"Amsterdam, hmm, I hear they are all about pleasure there…" I said, as he drew me closer.

"Oh you have never been? I'll have to take you and we will have the time of our lives." He drew my hand down as he began to suckle my neck.

All I could think about was that he was talking about us having a future together. Mrs. Dele Thompson, Mrs. Dele Thompson, it sounded so good in my head. I replayed it once more as I looked in his eyes, which were half closed with lust.

I relaxed and released all my inhibitions.

Oh my gawd!!!!
Oh my gaawd!!!
Oh, oh oh, MY GAAAWWD!!!

It was the most intense, amazing night of my life! Who would have known?

You see the ring was placed just right. So with every stroke it caused multiple explosions. We went three times in a row and finally we collapsed on his satin sheets.

That was the first time.

Since then three times in a night was just our standard. And for the record, each time was better than the last. I found myself thinking about him daily and looking forward to the nights when we planned to see each other.

Whenever he wanted to see me, he would messenger over a gift: a big box, always containing chocolates, a note saying when and where, and an expensive g-string. This time was no different. He sent me a black lacy La

Perla. It had only been two weeks and already I had about ten beautiful panties.

I met him at his house. He suggested ordering dinner, except we never did because we soon ended up in bed.

When we were done, he looked at me smugly. "I see you like…" I could hear the smile in his voice.

"I no fit lie…I like, I like!" I said, sighing with pleasure. I won't lie, I have been around the block more than a few times but I am telling you that every experience with Dele was certainly one for the books.

I was just beginning to snuggle up to him when he turned over to the mahogany carved bed stand that he had told me he bought in Abidjan and looked at his watch, a Cartier tank. Then he lifted himself up and rolled me off him.

"You know, you should really go."

"That's okay, I don't have any plans for the morning and I can spend the night."

"Well, babe, I have plans and I can't have you making me late." He handed me a towel. "If you like you can shower before you go."

I looked at him and then I looked at the towel. It was so plush that it reminded me of towels in the finer hotels. I sighed and got up. He sat back on the bed and watched me as I walked away. I could see him getting a little hot as he watched me, so I put a little extra switch in my step, just to remind him of what he was really missing.

As I walked into his huge shower, I thought about how to broach the subject of his bedside manner with him. He had never let me spend the night and he disliked coming to my house, said my sheets were too rough and he just felt more comfortable at his place. Well, I couldn't fault him there I thought as I turned on his shower. The various jets started hitting every part of my body. I enjoyed the sensation and tried to ignore the fact that what he had just done had made me feel like a common whore.

I was soaping myself up when I realized that he had gotten into the shower with me.

"I thought you might need help washing your back," he said, smiling mischievously. I guess I could wait till next time to tell him to change the way he spoke to me, because from the way he was touching me, I knew it was going to be one of those showers.

Amaka

Simulated Diamonds

I walked down Mina's driveway wearing my promise ring. Jeffrey had it appraised for the insurance; it was a two carat, round brilliant cut, very, very slightly included, E grade, almost colorless solitaire set in platinum.

I loved it.

I know I was supposed to keep everything under wraps but I couldn't put a ring like this in a drawer somewhere. I had to wear it, watch it catch the light. I had to show the world that I had the most wonderful man and that he loved me completely. Jeffrey giving me this ring erased every doubt I had in my mind. I knew that it would even shut Titi up. No married man goes around spending $10k on a ring for a woman. This was all the proof I needed.

When I stopped looking at the ring, I noticed Mina's garden. All her flowers were in bloom. I loved spring; everything looked better in the spring and Mina's garden was no exception. All the homes in her subdivision had well-groomed lawns but Mina's was immaculate. When it came to the home, she had a sense of style that was truly unparalleled.

Just as I was about to ring Mina's doorbell, Titi pulled up in a new Land Rover. It was black and sleek. I watched her exit the car, looking set in her Rock and Republic jeans and a very crisp white, well tailored shirt. It fit her like a glove and had this green piping and detailing. The green matched her Micheal Kors purse and Gucci sandals.

Like I said, she looked set.

"Na wa O! Titi, a new ride!" I hollered out to her. She smiled, struck a pose and said, "you know it," and then she started to walk up the cobblestone driveway to me. As she got closer I asked her what happened to her BMW.

"I traded it in. I got a great commission and I decided to treat myself."

"It's very nice," I said.

Titi raved, "Tell me about it! It has a navigation system and everything."

"Looks like real estate has been good to you."

"Well, we thank God," she said and I turned around to press the bell -- with my left hand.

Just as Mina opened the door, Titi let out a scream.

"What is that?" she screamed again. "What is that rock on your finger?!!!!"

Mina took my hand and looked at the stone intently.

"This is a high quality stone," she said. "Where is it from? Tiffany's?" She ushered us into the family room which she had changed around a little to reflect the spring season.

"Forget where it's from. Did Jeffrey give that to you?" Titi asked, still screaming.

Mina asked pointedly, "Did you get it appraised?"

"Yes, yes and yes!" I said, basking in their attention.

"So Jeffrey asked you to be his wife, wow!" Mina said. "It's only been a couple of months."

"So what, I guess when its right, its right!" Titi cried, surprisingly supportive.

I didn't want to dampen the excitement by telling them it was only a promise ring but I knew I had to tell them, otherwise they might go telling the world and it could affect Jeffrey's issues with his child's mother. I looked around and noticed the drapes had been changed and the sofas looked slip covered. I purposely kept my mind on the furniture so I wouldn't think about what I had to say.

"So how did he propose?" Mina asked as she sat down on a new ottoman. I loved what she was wearing.

"Was it in Brazil?" She was gesticulating wildly and the bell sleeves of her emerald green chiffon caftan made elegant sweeps through the air.

"Are you daydreaming or something?" Titi said, slapping my arm. Again I noticed the exquisite detailing on her shirt.

"Titi, that is a lovely shirt, where did you get it?" I asked.

"It is a Davida shirt; she is a designer in Lagos and her shirts are quite spectacular. But who is talking about shirts now, spill the beans, how did the man propose? Oh jare, I know it was romantic!" She prodded my shoulder with her red acrylic nail.

"It was on the plane home from Brazil," I started, while they looked at me expectantly.

"We were there in first class and the waitress had just given us a glass of champagne."

"Ah first class, the only way to fly," Mina interjected.

"So what did he say?" Titi prompted eagerly.

"Well, he told me that he loved me."

"How sweet," Titi sighed.

"And then he said that he wanted to spend the rest of his life with me," I continued hesitantly.

"And then he popped the question?" Titi jumped in.

"Well, not exactly." I lowered my voice.

"What do you mean not exactly?" Mina asked.

I had to admit it. "Well, he hasn't actually proposed yet."

"What do you mean?" Mina quizzed. "He gave you the ring, didn't he?"

"Yes, he did," I said, "but as a promise ring."

"A promise ring?" Mina and Titi asked in puzzled unison.

At that moment, I knew I shouldn't have worn the ring. "Well, you know he has a child already..." I started to rationalize.

"Ehen, and so what, why should that stop him from proposing?" Titi jumped in.

"It's not that it stops him, but he just has to tie up a few loose ends first," I said, quoting Jeffrey.

"So why couldn't he wait?" Mina said.

"I guess, because he's worried that I will lose faith in him."

Titi sighed. "This story get k-leg, there is something fishy about this."

I jumped up at her statement. "Madam Suspicion, there is nothing more to it than this. This ring cost upwards of ten thousand. No one spends that on a whim." I was almost tearful at this point. "Why can't you just be happy for me?"

"I am happy for you!" Titi said quickly, "but I am also your friend and I don't want to see you get hurt."

"Look, he is going back to Nigeria next week and when he gets there he is going to sort everything out, and when he gets back in about a month, he will officially propose and tell my parents and everything," I said, twisting my new ring nervously around my finger.

"Loose ends or not, something doesn't sound right at all, you sure say no be 419?" Titi reiterated.

"419?! Look Titi, what exactly are you trying to say, that a man like Jeffrey can't be interested in someone like me unless it's 419. I never expected you of all people to be so hateful."

I was so hurt by Titi's statement. More than once she had mentioned how handsome Jeffrey was and that such men are usually never unattached. She kept saying how a man like him could have his pick and I just ignored her but I felt sure she was implying that he wouldn't pick me.

"Amaka, I am not trying to be hateful, just cautious."

"Sounds like hate to me," I hissed.

"Ok, Amaka. Calm down, I am sure everything is going to be fine," Mina said. "Look Obinna has a vintage bottle of Dom Perignon that he has been saving for a special occasion, let me get it and we will truly celebrate. After all it's not every day that such a wonderful woman finds the love of her life! Abi!"

"Yes, O!" Titi shouted, a little too enthusiastically. She looked over at me and held out her hands towards me and said, "Still friends?"

I hugged her and smiled. "Of course," but deep down, I wondered.

"Voila, the champagne!" Mina announced triumphantly.

"Won't he be upset if you take it?" Titi said.

"Don't worry about Obinna, I know how to handle him." She popped the cork and we sipped this most delicious champagne and looked over bridal magazines that Mina suddenly pulled out of somewhere, proclaiming that she didn't care when the proposal came, that as far as she was concerned, she had a wedding to plan.

And so the evening went, filled with champagne, jollof rice and our dear Vera Wang.

Later on that night, my mother called. I knew it was her before looking at the caller ID because she is the only one that calls at all hours of the night. She might call at 1 am my time because she woke up at 6 and my father wasn't up yet. I heard her talking to my answering machine.

"Hello, Haay low! Amaka, answer the phone! Are you sleeping? Haay low, Amaka, answer the phone, I know you are there because no daughter of mine can be out at this time, after 1 in the morning, Haba! Haay Low!"

Finally I decided to answer the phone which was my first mistake; I guess I was still giddy about the ring.

"Hello Mummy."

"Ehen, Amaka, why did it take you so long to answer?"

"I was sleeping Mummy."

"Okay, it is only 1 am; shebi, you are awake now."

"Yes."

"Okay, good, call me back, my credit will soon finish."

So I went fishing for a phone card to call her back. As I listened to the mechanical voice telling me I had ten minutes, I was thankful that whatever stress she was bringing wouldn't last very long.

"Amaka, I have been praying for you, have you been doing the prayers I sent you?" she asked.

"Yes Mummy." I lied, her prayers were long and convoluted and I preferred to talk to God in my own way.

"You know that Pastor Johnson?" My mum and her pastors, I guess she is like those Hollywood women and their gurus. Unfortunately I remembered Pastor Johnson, how could I forget?

I met him last Christmas when I went home to Lagos for the holidays. I went home to see my parents and my brother. My mother had wanted me home so she could launch Operation FIND HUBBY. Mission was to find me a husband. She attacked it from all angles.

Physically, she put me on a diet. It was what I call a stare-down diet. Basically she would stare me down every time I went to eat something that she considered unacceptable. Bread got a stare and a shake of the head. A second helping of rice got a stare followed by heavy breathing. Ice cream got a stare, heavy breathing and finally a "no wonder you are getting so fat!" It was quite effective I must say, because I lost ten pounds.

And then came the emotional tactics, she spent hours lecturing me about lowering my expectations. "Fairytales only exist in books," she would say and then go on and on, elaborating the point. So far, not so bad, I could deal with that. It was the spiritual angle I couldn't deal with.

That was how I met Pastor Johnson. He was the leader of the Strong Prayers for Signs and Wonders prayer group. He did prayers for a fee, but naturally he called it an offering.

One morning I woke up to see them in my living room.

"Ehen Amaka, you are up, come here and greet Pastor and the sisters."

Like an obedient daughter, I curtsied to them while uttering greetings. I thought that would be it and started to wander back to my bedroom. My mum called me back sharply.

"Do you know that when this man prays, heaven opens for him?"

I looked at her blankly thinking okay, should I care? Her smile told me I was in trouble.

"I have asked him to come and pray for your marriage!"

I was mortified. Was I now a case for local prayer groups? I swear you would have thought I was leprous and blind in one eye, the way my mother carried on. More than once I wondered if my issues with men had less to do with my physical looks and so called pickiness, and more with the sort of emotional insecurity that having a mom like mine creates.

Anyway at that point I was backed into a corner so I felt I had no choice but to kneel down before Pastor Johnson and his backup prayer girls. They formed a circle around me and started chanting. It was completely weird. My mom who normally wouldn't even go into a Pentecostal church (she called them clap-clap churches and much preferred her sedate Anglican service) was here kowtowing to this charlatan and buying into this wearing white nonsense. How had the situation gotten so bad? I wondered.

Meanwhile Pastor Johnson and his girls were swaying in a supposed trance. "Help this young girl to see the bone of her bone," he sang. "Help her, help her, Lord," the girls chanted after him. "Help her to learn how to be a wife." "Help her, help her, Lord."

He sang variations on the theme and while they seemed quite harmless, for some reason I decided to open my eyes and check what was going on. Pastor Johnson had positioned himself in front of me and was peering down the front of my shirt with a hungry look in his eyes. I grabbed my pajama top and pulled it close while glaring at him.

That was when he launched into attack mode: "Aha, I see the problem O!" He started to shake and shimmy, I guess it was some prophetic disco move! "This girl does not believe," he announced, finally stopping. "Your enemies are using her unbelief to block her blessings," he continued. His girls gave appropriate sighs and moans.

My mother shrugged her shoulders in an 'ehen, I knew it' gesture. Then the 'help hers' came in earnest. They started swirling around me in a faster rhythm: "Help this girl, Lord!" Help her unbelief, Lord!" Help her foolishness, Lord!" Help her stupidity, Lord!" Then out of nowhere, he gave me a dirty slap: "Help her stubbornness, Lord."

Chineke! I jumped up in anger, which kind yeye pastor?! He stood there in defiance. My mother started begging me to return to my knees, but I had had enough. I told her she could kneel in my place if she wanted to but as for me I was going to my room and if she didn't move from my way, I would call my father who I knew wouldn't stand for this nonsense. Knowing this too, she quickly moved out of my way and started apologizing to the Pastor, who began to tell her that I was a special case and would require three times more money than had been previously arranged in order for him to go to the mountain and do deep prayers for me. I was so mad.

"Well, do you remember him?" she probed.

"Yes," I said. "What about him?"

"He was in the paper last month. The man was just a thief. Imagine they say he has been sleeping with various girls in exchange for helping them find a husband or get pregnant, can you just imagine that?"

As I thought about him leering down my pajama top, I could more than imagine.

"Well, he was a fake, but I have found this new pastor. Everyone says he is a true man of God. When you come back this Christmas, I will take you to see him. He has shunned all material life, just takes a donation that he gives to charity, his shrine is deep in the bush."

Oh hell no, I shook my head and started to protest, but then I realized, why bother? I have a ring on my finger, and by Christmas, Jeffrey would have sorted himself out and we would be able to announce our engagement to the world and my mum!

As if on cue, my calling card announced I only had one minute left. I quickly ended the conversation and lay back down on my bed. I was going to sleep well jare; I was going to be a wife!

Titi

That's what friends are for

Which kind microwave love be dis now?! Haba! I know Maksy was in love, but my darling Amaka can be pretty naïve when it comes to men. The girl can wrestle with organic chemistry but as far as human chemistry goes, she fails every time.

Now it's not as if I don't wish Maksy the best and I know that Jeffrey makes her happy, but something about that man concerns me. It's like he is too damn smooth. Never even told her he had a kid and then this expensive promise ring, and what exactly is he going to sort out back in Nigeria?

I was thinking all these thoughts and planning how I was going to conduct my investigation into Oga Jeffrey when the phone rang.

It was my Dele.

"Hi, sweetheart," I answered.

"Hi, Titi."

Funny thing, no matter how many nights we shared and how many times I used a term of endearment with him, the only thing he ever called me was Titi.

"Titi, I need you to find me a house."

"Really?" I cooed. "What kind of place? A cozy cottage for two?" I joked, lacing my voice with much honey.

"No, actually I'm in the market for a home," he said. "I'm thinking of settling down."

Settling down? I thought about Amaka's ring. It had only been a few weeks but the sex was fantastic and we did get along fairly well. Could proposals be in the air for everyone?

"Settling down huh," I said, playing it cool. "...and what kind of house, would you care to settle down into?"

"I'm thinking six bedrooms, master on main, finished terrace level, media room, gourmet kitchen, you know, the works."

I sat up. Now he was really speaking my language. I went into business mode instantly.

"Square footage?" I asked.

"Over 7000."

"Neighborhood?"

"I'd like to get more bang for my buck. It doesn't have to be the city, but a decent place, maybe a country club setting."

"Anything else?" I asked.

"Yes, I need somewhere grand, and at least 2 acres."

"Ok, I'll get to work."

"Think you can find me a place?" Dele asked.

"Do you come every time? " I asked back.

"He laughed. "Every single time!"

"I'll call you with the details," I said. My mind was already racing at the possibilities. A house just for us...I would find him the best deal possible!

"Oh and Titi?" he continued, "Let's meet tonight, I am sending you a package."

I smiled and hung up.

The FedEx man came by almost immediately after. It was perfectly synchronized.

I looked inside: Godiva chocolates, and a g-string with ruffles and satin ribbon. The note read: The Georgian Terrace, eight pm.

Mina

Confrontation

I decided I had no other choice than to confront the little bitch. After she saw me and how classy and beautiful I was, she would know Obinna would never leave me for her and was just using her for sex. Probably deviant sex that no self respecting woman could be expected to do, certainly not a lady like myself.

I went to Obinna's hospital and I even dressed for the part. I put on a wig and sunglasses because the last thing I needed was for someone to recognize me. Even though I rarely went there, I was sure I would be easily remembered.

So I donned a chestnut brown wig and put on non-descript clothes, and went to check out this Carolina person. My plan wasn't very concrete so I ended up in the cafeteria, strategizing.

Suddenly, who walked in but Obinna and some woman. From the way he was holding her and how affectionate they were being, it was clear to me that this must be Carolina. He wasn't even being discreet. How dare he expose us like this? People in this hospital know he is married and here he is cavorting in public with the help!

She was nothing to write home about. She wasn't ugly but definitely could not compete with me in the looks department. For starters she was very dark with short hair, and she was overweight. Not grossly so, but she clearly hadn't seen a gym in quite some time.

She brought out some dishes from a lunch bag and he rubbed his hands together and licked his lips in anticipation. When she opened the plates, the aroma of the food practically stopped all the conversation in the cafeteria. It smelled amazing, like fried rice and goat meat with moin-moin and fried plantain. No wonder Obinna has been putting on a few extra pounds lately.

He dug in with gusto and while they ate, they conversed happily. I couldn't hear what they were saying but from the snatches that I caught, I realized they were speaking in Ibo.

I became a little alarmed. Was she some plant that Obinna's mother had sent to uproot me? I pushed down the paranoia and continued to watch them. He finished his food and then squeezed her thigh and kissed her on the lips. Then he put on his white coat and left.

She started to gather up the dishes like the maid that she was. I decided this was the best time to approach her.

"Hello," I said to her.

"Hello." She looked up at me smiling curiously. Her Nigerian accent was quite pronounced.

"Your food smelled wonderful," I said, trying to put her at ease.

"Thank you. I like to cook."

"Are you a nurse?" I asked.

"Oh no," she said. "In fact, I just got my CNA certification. I am a nursing assistant."

"Oh, do you go to university for that?" I said, playing dumb.

"No oh, University, I have never been. My family is pretty poor back in Nigeria, where I am from, so I was not able to go to school."

"My name is Patricia," I said, extending my hand.

"My name is Carolina." She took my hand.

"Was that your husband?" I asked.

"No," she said meekly, looking off at the swinging doors of the cafeteria.

"Your boyfriend?" I probed.

"Yes," she replied.

"Is he a doctor?" I asked, resisting the urge to slap the taste of goat meat out of her mouth.

"Yes, I don't know what he saw in me. I guess it's the cooking and the loving," she said.

"You love him?" I asked, trying to hide my disdain.

"Yes, he is such a nice man," she smiled. I felt sick.

"So why don't you marry him?" I asked.

"Maybe soon," Carolina said.

At which point the bile had risen into my throat and I just hauled off and slapped her. She fell out of her chair because she was taken completely by surprise.

"So you want to marry another woman's husband?!"

People were looking at us now.

"Listen, you little bitch, if you know what is good for you, you will leave my husband alone!" I screamed and since I noticed the security guard coming, I picked up my Vuitton purse and stalked out, leaving the stupid girl crying on the floor.

I got home and paced the room. I was waiting for Obinna. I was going to give him an ultimatum: drop that bitch and I might consider not divorcing you. I know men like to play around and I was willing to overlook this little slip, providing he was appropriately contrite.

I was not prepared for what happened next.

I had settled in my mind how things were going to play out. Obinna was probably shaking in his shoes now he knew I had found out his little secret, and he would come back and beg for my forgiveness. I would hold out for a while and then after he had suffered adequately, I would relent.

I was soaking in my tub, listening to Sade to relax myself when I heard the front door slam shut. I was not surprised to hear his footsteps on the stairs, it sounded like he was rushing up. I thought he was rushing to beg me not to leave. I got out of the tub, put on my robe and sat on the stool in front of my mirror. Just then he burst in through the door.

"So you think you can go around slapping people eh?!" he shouted, and with that he slapped me with such force that I fell to the ground like Carolina had hours earlier.

I held my cheek in shock and looked at him. He was enraged. This was not what I had planned. Where was the contrite spirit? The pleading for forgiveness?

Obinna started to yell: "You idiot, I should have left you a long time ago. You dare to put your hands on my woman."

At that point I found my voice.

"Your woman? I am your wife, you are calling that bitch your woman?"

"Watch your mouth, Mina, you don't even know her. If anyone is a bitch, it's you and you are a cold-hearted one to boot."

With that retort he walked into my closet and started to throw my clothes out onto the floor.

"What are you doing?" I asked, following him into the large walk-in closet.

"I want you out of this house by tonight."

I was in shock. "This is my house, are you crazy?" I screamed indignantly.

"Your house huh, when was the last time you paid a bill in this house?"

"I made you. You bastard! I made you. Without me, you would have been nothing!" I cried.

"You didn't make me, I worked for this shit. I busted my butt every day, studying, working, learning and now I am the best doctor that I could be and you had nothing to do with that!" Obinna yelled, suddenly looking less like the spineless fool I had thought him.

"I pushed you to do better," I countered.

"I was already in medical school when I met you, so what exactly did you do?"

"I showed you the finer things in life, without me you would have been a rinky dink doctor, living a rinky dink life. You bastard, I gave you everything I had and this is how you treat me."

Then out of nowhere I began to cry. Images of every man who had ever abandoned or hurt me flashed before my eyes: Obinna, Uncle Tosan, my father. I sat on the bed and then I began to howl.

Even in the midst of all the drama and anger, Obinna still found it in himself to be compassionate. He stopped, holding a silk cavialli blouse in his hand.

He looked at me and sighed. "Mina, I'm sorry, I am just not happy anymore, I haven't been for a long time. I met Carolina at work. It was innocent, one day I smelled her lunch and I asked her if she catered and then one thing led to another. She is the sweetest woman I have ever known. She makes me happy and life is peaceful with her."

I was heartbroken and this fool was talking about happiness.

"I guess water always finds its own level," I said, wiping my tears. "You were never good enough for me anyway."

"Whatever, Mina," he said, his voice hardening again. "I gave this relationship everything I had. You were the one holding back. I married you even though I was under a lot of pressure from my family not to. I believed in you and you gave me nothing in return. No love, no support, you just wanted to ride my back into your fantasy life. Well this horse has had enough! I have already talked to a lawyer, I want a divorce."

Haba, I was beginning to see that Obinna had really grown wings. Well, he was not going to fly away just like that!

"Oh you'll get a divorce and by the time I am done with you, you won't even a penny to your name," I screamed.

"Look, I suggest you don't try anything funny, you will get what is fair and that's all," he said pointedly.

"That's all? I made you, Obinna. Without me you would have been nothing!" I cried in frustration.

Obinna started to laugh. "Without you, I would have been happy and for the record what did you really add to my life? What?! he shouted.

"Please tell me, how did you make me? I was already on my way to becoming a doctor when you met me and for your information, I am damn good at it. The only thing you showed me was how to live a lie, trying to forget where you came from!"

"I can't believe you are being such a bastard," I said weakly.

He laughed again, "I guess, it takes one to know one. Look Mina, we are calling it quits, so let's skip all this drama. You just move out ASAP."

"I am not going anywhere," I said defiantly.

"Well, you have a choice, either you go quietly or you go in disgrace."

Was he threatening me? With what? "You are the one who will have the disgrace, you are the adulterer."

"Well, an adulterer is better than a prostitute any day."

"What did you say?"

"You heard me, I know all about your sordid past and if you push me, all your little society friends will know too."

I was shocked into silence

"Why are you quiet? You thought no one knew? Well that which was hidden has been brought to light. I know you were an escort in NY. So if you don't want everyone to know about your life as a prostitute then you better behave yourself." Obinna picked up his jacket.

"Remember, I want you out of this house, I'll give you till the end of the week. Furthermore let me warn you. Do not come near Carolina again. If you so much as speak a bad word to her, I will cause you serious pain because she is not only a sweet, gentle woman, she is also about to be the mother of my child."

All I could do was look at him in shock.

He walked out of the room and through my tears I noticed the imprint his Ferragamo loafers made on the plush beige carpet. I had bought him those shoes.

I sat down on the tufted leather ottoman in the dressing area of our closet, looked around at the luxurious space, all maple wood and mauve and green silk print, and began to weep.

Amaka

Lover's Rock

Those few days leading up to Jeffrey's return to Nigeria were bittersweet; he had finished his coursework and was returning home. We had talked about the future extensively and had tentatively decided that he would sort things out at home and then return here, after which we would take that next big step.

Jeffrey was wonderfully sweet in those last days. We packed up his apartment together. He had several suitcases, a couple of which he had already packed before I got there. But he had accumulated so much stuff in his six months in Atlanta that he had to leave a few things at my place, like a beautiful, limited edition William Johnson print entitled *Self Portrait with Pipe.* Jeffrey had purchased the print because I told him it reminded me of him. The gentleman in the picture is wearing a smoking jacket and has just lit a pipe. The expression on his face is stern and perhaps arrogant but yet there is a sweetness in him. When Jeffrey hung it in my living room, he kissed me and said: "It is a poor substitution but think of me when you see it and before you know it, you'll be back in my arms."

His imminent departure felt so surreal, like it was happening in a movie. I was trying to steel myself because I knew how much I would miss him. I felt a little bit ridiculous because I was acting as if we had been together forever, and it had just been a few months. Yet in that time, Jeffrey had become such an integral part of my life. I couldn't imagine spending my days without him. We had settled into such a routine: half the time we spent the night at my house and the other half at his place. Since the first night we had hooked up, we hadn't slept separately.

I found myself volleying between joy and pain -- joy that I had finally met the man I was going to spend my life with, pain that he was leaving. When he touched me, it was just like all the songs say it would be…electric. We clicked on so many levels. I knew I made him happy, and he definitely did the same for me.

When we had finally packed up Jeffrey's life here, shipped or stored his things as necessary, Jeffrey suggested that we spend his last weekend at the W hotel. At first I was reluctant. I wanted us to stay at my place, where I could cook a special meal and where we could just generally be at home. He insisted by telling me that he had already reserved a suite and he wanted us to spend every available minute enjoying one another, not focusing on the minutiae of day to day living.

So we went to the W. We got there Friday evening and his flight was Sunday afternoon. I had packed quickly but I had remembered to bring my swimsuit and a very sexy Frederick's baby doll piece which Titi had given me for my last birthday, along with a card in which she had written: "Enjoy…for once."

We had meant to go down to Savu for dinner but as I was unpacking, Jeffrey saw my Kama Sutra set of edible lotions and potions, feather included. I had ordered it when he told me he was going back home. The idea was to make sure he remembered who and what he was leaving behind. Once he took the feather out and started to tickle me suggestively, Savu was long forgotten. We opted for late night room service instead while we worked up an appetite.

Mina

The Doctors' Wives Club

I had been dreading this party for days, but I couldn't get out of it. It was a baby shower for Chichi, the newest wife in our group. Titi calls us the Doctors' Wives Club. In truth we don't have a club, it just so happens that most of us who are married to Nigerian doctors and don't work hang out together. But it's not just any doctor's wife that is part of our clique. Most of our husbands are high earners; either they are specialists like Obinna or they have their own practices. In any case, we often get together to have lunch and chat about our families and lives.

There is a little bit of 'keeping up with the Joneses' that goes on in our group. For instance, Yetunde and her husband just moved to a beautiful house over in Dunwoody. The house was valued at over $3 million. Almost immediately, Ronke started pressuring her husband to move out of their Stone Mountain mansion which, by all accounts, was beautiful and in Smoke Rise

Country Club. She wanted to move to Buckhead and had her eye set on what she called a 'simple home.' A simple home with nine bedrooms, a swimming pool and a tennis court!

Never mind that Yetunde was one of the few wives who worked. She was a partner at one of the midsized law firms, and Ronke had never worked a day in her life. Anyway Ronke and family moved too and got a new Mercedes to boot, end result being that Ronke's husband is called the shift troll because in spite of his good income, his monthly burn is so outrageous that he has to troll various hospitals moonlighting for extra cash.

We had been meeting at Nonye's house when it was decided that we were going to throw a shower for Chichi. Chichi hadn't been able to make it that afternoon, so we planned it as a surprise. Initially I hadn't wanted to take the lead, but since Nonye kept making little remarks about my childless state, I decided to try and act like being childless was by choice not circumstance. So I decided to throw Chichi the most talked about shower of the year. It wouldn't be just jollof rice and sitting around in a living room like Nonye typically does, I would show them what real class and style was.

I hired EventSavvy, an ultra hip event design company, and we came up with a Lunch at Tiffany's theme. Chichi was having a baby girl so it was all diamonds and divas. It was also going to be a Jack and Jill baby shower; the men would be inside having cigars and cognac while the ladies would be having a refined lunch in the backyard.

I had forgotten about the party until the night before when Sophie, the event planner, arrived with the tents and rented chairs for the backyard. She and her team proceeded to set up the space. They had tiny little tees embellished with rhinestones hung up on a clothesline, welcoming the newest diva to the world. I just stood there in my La Perla silk robe and watched. I couldn't do anything else. Just moments before the doorbell rang, I had been lying in bed, willing myself to sleep. I had just been about to take an Ambien when Sophie and team arrived. She was a little surprised to see me in my robe considering it was only 7 pm, but she was discreet as usual and just went right to work.

I watched them decorate my backyard with paper lanterns and thought about my husband. I hadn't spoken to him since our confrontation. He had sent me an email saying he didn't want me to be out on the street so I could stay in the house for now, he would find somewhere else to stay. I found myself grateful for that small kindness even though I knew he was staying with Carolina. He had, however, limited my access to our accounts, so I had barely enough to cover the costs for this party. I found myself unable to do the necessary things: contact a divorce lawyer, face reality. I was in a state of shock. I had no idea how to do what needed to be done, so at this moment it was easier to focus on simple issues like where the flowers should go and whether to serve cake or petit fours.

My life was falling apart and here I was thinking like Martha Stewart. What was I going to do tomorrow when everyone was here? Would they already know about Obinna and me? Would Nonye laugh in my face? What about that little bit of nastiness that Obinna mentioned…would he spread that around too?

Sophie walked up to me with little baby champagne bottles in her hands. Baby Veuve Cliquot. She was thinking of making them part of the centerpiece. I looked at her and smiled. Champagne and flowers! If only life could be so bubbly and smell so sweet!

Titi

A dream home

I had been scouring the listings to find Dele the perfect spot. I had found a few places that were nice but he wanted something quite dramatic. Then I came across this place. It was resort style living in Georgia!

I had to check it out. The model home was pure grandeur. Totally Dele, I thought. It was all waterfalls and marble walkways. The detailing was exquisite. Each home would have the extras like a lavishly landscaped backyard and pool. The master suite was like a dream, your own personal fantasy.

It was a brand new subdivision breaking ground at between eight hundred thousand and three million. I knew it was not only beautiful but it was a good deal. For a million five, you could get some beautiful homes in Atlanta, but this was absolutely spectacular. So I called Dele immediately. Even though I knew this was pretty much what he wanted, I decided to show him some other houses as well.

We planned to meet the next day after I contacted him because Dele was very eager to find a place and close the deal. I agreed to take him out in the morning because of the baby shower at Mina's at four that evening. We went to the first house, which was in the Buckhead area of Atlanta. He loved the area but didn't feel it was grand enough.

Then we went to a beautiful house on the well- known Riverside Drive. It definitely had curb appeal and he seemed to like it. In fact, it seemed to turn him on. By the time we reached the master suite, he pulled me to him and I could feel that he was hard so when he whispered throatily in my ear, "Are we alone?" I understood where this was going. He put his hand up my skirt and reveled in how ready I was. Then right there in front of the marble wet bar, he bent me over and took me from behind.

I could see his face in the mirror, and the expression was strangely not of love or joy as I had imagined it would be. I had thought he would be so overwhelmed at the thought of sharing this home with me. Instead the look on his face was one of triumph, after something has been conquered. I found it disturbing so I closed my eyes and pictured us hosting a party together in this space. Maybe our engagement party; I came immediately.

Afterwards, while he was making himself presentable, I kissed him. He looked at me and smiled. "What was that for?"

"For changing my life," I responded.

He raised his eyebrows and nodded imperceptibly. "Let's go" he said abruptly. "You said you had one more house?"

We arrived at the subdivision in record time, there was absolutely no traffic. Dele wasn't that impressed with the neighborhood. As we were going down the I-20, known as the black side of town, he said he preferred something more multicultural, meaning whiter, but I persevered. This particular area was an African-American enclave of professionals and business people. It was where the black upper-middle class called home. I looked at it this way: It really wasn't that far from downtown and since one would probably put the kids in private school anyway, the quality of the schools in the neighborhood was irrelevant.

When we got to the estate, I knew I had hit a home run from Dele's expression. A typical Nigerian, he wanted everyone to know he had arrived and this estate said you had not only arrived, but in serious style. Dele began to murmur to himself: "this was exactly what I had in mind." He also liked the fact that it was new construction which would allow him to really tailor the house to his style—my style too I thought gleefully to myself. Once we had checked out the place, Dele was sold and declared he was ready to sign on the dotted line immediately.

"Aah, aah, Dele, are you sure? What's the hurry?" I said.

"Look, Titi, I am a man with minimal time to waste so when I see something I like, I go for it immediately." Dele said this while looking intently into my eyes. I could feel my panties get moist again.

I know, I know… I am a total slut!

Amaka

Au revoir

Saying goodbye is always hard. Saying goodbye to the man you love is heart-wrenching. I walked Jeffrey to the security check area and we embraced a last time before he went in. It was a long sweet hug. I buried my face in his shoulder and inhaled his cologne, trying to imprint it on my mind forever. He kissed me and stroked my cheek. "I love you, Amaka, always know that this is true. You are the love of my life."

He kissed the tears that were beginning to well up and trickle out of my eyes.

"Stop," he said softly. "Don't make this harder for me than it is already."

I couldn't speak.

"I'll be back before you know it."

This is a boarding announcement. Northwest Flight number 501 to Amsterdam will begin boarding in 10 minutes. Please proceed to the gate at this time.

I considered trying to make him miss his flight, but he pulled away from me and began to walk through security. He turned just before he walked through the metal detector and blew me a kiss, causing people to turn and stare. I smiled at him and when he had gone through, I walked to the parking lot alone, dejected.

When I got into my car, I pulled down the mirror and fixed my face. I was going to miss my sweetheart but he would soon be back and then we would never have to be separated again.

I pulled out of my parking stall and headed to Mina's house, fantasizing about the day when they would be throwing me a baby shower. If it was a boy, I could name him Jeffrey Junior and a girl, well that was easy…I had always loved the name Kanwulia…it meant let us rejoice, and we would call her KK for short.

Mina

No sweat

It was a difficult day. I got up, showered and got dressed. I was going for a soft, sexy but don't take no shit look, in other words...Gabrielle Union meets Cleopatra Jones. So I chose a cream knit halter and chocolate linen pants which I paired with lizard skin stiletto slippers. I brushed my hair till it fell in shiny waves on my shoulders and then I put on just a hint of makeup. I took a look in the mirror and for the first time in a few days, I smiled at the result.

I was a beautiful woman. I had a thought that Obinna would come to the party, see me and immediately come to his senses. Child or no child, he would want me back. I had even wrapped my mind around the fact that he was about to have a child with another woman; I could deal with it, after all is he the first man to have a baby out of wedlock? The important thing was to keep my marriage. I was the rightful wife.

As I looked in the mirror, my resolve strengthened. This was just a challenge and we would get through it. I knew deep down that Obinna still loved me; why else would he say that I could stay in the house, which, by the way, I had no intention of moving out of. He must have realized that Carolina or whatever her name was could not offer him all I had to give him: class and style. Could she organize the kind of party that I was throwing today? Could she have the crème de la crème of the Atlanta Nigeria society in her house just by making a few calls? No one would accept her and he would be shunned by his own community. Even he wouldn't take that chance.

I walked downstairs and was amazed to see the transformation. Normally my home was quite beautiful, but today it had become a vision in sage and pink. Vibrant pink peonies and beautiful, sage green hydrangeas were overflowing from vases dotted around the house. The Chef and his staff were bustling about in the kitchen, while Sophie and her girls put finishing touches on the outside space. It was quite breathtaking. Chichi would be so happy and Nonye -- well, she could eat her heart out.

Sophie gave me a little wave when she saw me and started to walk inside. She pinned a corsage on me when she got close enough and offered me a drink; it was a frozen, pale pink concoction with a mint leaf garnish.

"What is this?" I asked.

"A bella bellini. The signature drink for this evening. It's made with champagne."

I took a sip. "It's delicious! Sophie dear, you have out done yourself."

"Well, you are a woman of great taste," she replied, smiling, "so I knew I had to bring my A game."

"Well, that you did."

"Come and taste the dishes Chef John is preparing," Sophie said as she pulled me to the kitchen.

Hours passed quickly and before I knew it, people started arriving for the shower. They were all met at the door by waiters serving the bella bellinis and hor d'oeuvres. My guests started oohing and aahing right away: "Oh Mina, you have really done it." "You have totally charged, I see!" While they were congratulating me on the party, Sophie was discreetly passing out her business cards.

Amaka and Titi walked in at almost the same time, Amaka looking a little morose while Titi looked like the cat that got the cream.

"Mina, darling. You no gree O! You no gree!" Titi said, raving in broken English as she always did when excited.

"It really looks lovely," Amaka concurred.

I was suddenly so glad to see them that I gave them a group hug. Titi looked a little taken aback; it was a bit out of character for me.

"Come on in," I said after releasing them, ignoring the shock in Titi's eyes and the concern in Amaka's. I led them through the living room to the back yard, where the other women were seated at tables laid with sage tablecloths with green chiffon overlays. Just as I finished seating them, Chichi and her husband arrived. She began to crying almost immediately. Her husband rubbed her shoulders affectionately and explained: "I think it's the hormones." She just shook her head and kept bawling.

The women quickly gathered her into their midst offering cooing sounds of encouragement while the men laughed and made merry with her husband, quickly settling him with a glass of cognac. He laughed heartily, the laugh of a father to be. A few of the guys asked me where Obinna was. I responded with a vague, "You doctors, always some emergency!" That seemed to stop the questions especially as they were distracted by a soccer match on the TV.

I moved between the men and the women, playing the hostess with the mostess. Eventually the party started winding down. The guys had eaten their fill and were just generally chilling, waiting for their wives. Chichi was opening her last present. I was finally feeling like everything had turned out quite well and then it happened:

Obinna walked in the front door with that girl on his arm and she was clearly pregnant and wearing an engagement ring.

Titi

Katakata

Na serious kwanta be dis O!

The whole party was abuzz. Mina's husband walked in with some other woman and from the looks of it, she was pregnant with his child! I looked around frantically for Mina. I knew things were really bad when I saw her quickly retreat upstairs without putting up a fight.

Obinna, though he looked a little taken aback, simply started introducing the woman he was with to everyone. It was really awkward, no one knew how to react, whether to be friendly or hostile... Chichi and her husband were the first to make their excuses. They left quickly and others followed. Some of the women tried to go upstairs to find Mina, but Amaka and I blocked the way. I made it clear from the look on my face that this was a no-go area.

As soon as the room was empty, Amaka and I faced Obinna.

"How could you do this?" Amaka started.

"Which kind wahala be dis eh!" I said.

Obinna looked a little contrite. "I sent Mina a text message telling her that we would be coming by to get some things. It's not my fault she never responded."

"So you decided that it was best to come to your marital home with another woman?" I shouted, pointing at Carolina who had been standing quietly behind Obinna. She looked like she wanted to fade into the walls.

"Look, this wasn't intentional. I forgot she was hosting something but anyway people had to know sooner or later. I guess this wasn't the best way to do it, but I am not ashamed of Carolina."

I bared my teeth like a lioness protecting her cubs,

"You should be ashamed, foolish man, opening your yansh for the world to see! You think it's Mina that looks bad here? It is you flaunting your whore in her face!" I lost my temper.

"You don't even know what is going on and you are here insulting me in my own house!" Obinna shouted back.

"This is Mina's house, too!" I said.

"Not for long."

"Oh really! Well, I know some good lawyers and by the time she is finished with you, let's see if that gold digger will still wants you!"

"Titi, it is enough," Amaka pleaded with me.

"No it is not. Someone needs to give this fool the truth," I said.

Obinna looked ready to explode, but instead he started to laugh: "I guess I should be glad she at least has true friends. But enough with this charade, you guys know Mina has never loved me. If anyone is a gold digger then it's her. She only wanted me for the life I could provide. This woman here loves me for me. Even if I couldn't give her all this," he said, motioning to the house, "it wouldn't matter to her." Obinna pulled Carolina towards him. She came meekly.

"And as for fighting me in a divorce, you better tell your friend not to try anything. I will give her what is fair, but if she tries to be mercenary, I will tell the world her secret!"

Carolina spoke for the first time, softly, "Nna anyi, there is no need to fight, let us go." She rubbed her hand on his shoulder gently, looking down at the floor.

Obinna acquiesced immediately and they walked together towards the door.

As soon as he left, Amaka and I started up the stairs.

We found Mina in her bathroom and she was a pile of tears, silk and chocolate linen.

Amaka

Even the strong cry

My heart went out to Mina. She looked so unlike herself, with mascara running down her face. Titi and I helped her to the bed. She did not stop weeping.

For a while, we just held her and whispered words of comfort while she wept. When she had stopped crying so hard, we asked her what was going on.

Titi spoke first: "Mina, what is happening, why didn't you tell us?"

Mina just shrugged her shoulders.

"I just couldn't…I couldn't tell anyone."

"Well, we are here now," I said. "How can we help?"

"How long has this been going on?" Titi asked. "Who is that girl?!"

"I don't know, I just found out about a month ago. I confronted her and then Obinna told me he was leaving me for her and that she was pregnant by him."

"No, now. It's not possible; Obinna cannot leave you." I said, trying to placate her.

"Are you blind?" she spat. "He has left me already.

"These gold digging sluts," Titi spat.

"She apparently came over recently from Nigeria," Mina continued.

"These Naija sluts!" Titi repeated.

"I know," Mina said. "I don't know how I could have been so blind." Tears began rolling down her cheeks afresh. "How could I let someone like that take my husband?"

"You can't blame yourself," I said.

"Yeah, blame that slut!"

"Titi, enough with the sluts," I countered.

"Why? That is what she is! Probably opened her legs and was cooking egusi for him." Titi was all riled up. "I told you, those damn Ngozis!"

"So what are you going to do now?" I asked, turning back to Mina.

"What can I do, I am at his mercy."

Titi ranted, "What do you mean at his mercy? He is the one that cheated on you! Thank God this is America, my dear; you can finish him in court. I know a very good lawyer, he helped one of my clients and believe me she is living the high life now."

"I can't do that," Mina said.

"What! Are you feeling sorry for the bastard?" Titi exclaimed.

"No, it's just that…" Mina faltered.

"Obinna has some hold over you, doesn't he? Knows some secret?" I said.

Mina nodded her head.

"Mina, this is your life. Regardless of anything, you were this man's wife, you were with him during the lean times and now that he has made something out of himself, he wants to dump you! I don't think so…Secret or not, you have to go for yours!" Titi argued.

I tried to be more gentle, "Mina, whatever it is, it can't be so bad. We all have skeletons in the closet."

Titi and I waited in silence for Mina to respond. I continued to rub her back while Titi paced the room.

Suddenly Mina let out a loud sob: "I used to be an escort!"

We all fell silent. I was shocked; I definitely hadn't expected this. I looked at Mina, perfect Mina. I just couldn't wrap my head around that she would sleep with men for money.

"You were a prostitute?" Titi said aghast.

Mina shook her head. "No, I was just an escort. But everyone will think I was a prostitute. I never slept with any of the guys."

"Really?" Titi's eyebrow rose involuntarily.

Mina was firm. "Yes. It was back when we were in college. Money was tight and I just did it for one summer. Quite a few girls were doing it then."

"Back in college… You were always carrying Louis Vuitton. Is that how you paid for all your nice stuff?" Titi asked.

"I know, my values were pretty screwed up then but I couldn't let anyone know my real situation," Mina sniffled.

I just looked at her in wonder. Mina had always claimed to be from some rich Nigerian family. She had said that her father had died and left her and her mum very well off. So in school she was always carrying the latest and we all envied her. Now it seemed she had been lying the whole time!

"Mina, na wa O," Titi said, shaking her head. I felt slightly angry with her for being so judgmental, but I didn't say anything.

"I know, I am so ashamed," Mina said. "No one can know…" she looked at us frantically, seeking reassurance, "…or I won't be able to show my face again."

"So this is what Obinna is holding over you?" Titi asked.

Mina nodded shamefaced. I stayed silent, still digesting it all.

"Okay well, let's talk damage control," Titi finally said. "Truth be told, you can't show your face even now, Mina, because believe me, everyone is going to be talking about what happened here tonight. So you better just find some inner strength and face the situation head on.

"As for divorcing Obinna, as far as I am concerned, you should still fight for what's yours. So what if he tells the world your secret? Half those women out there have done worse. As far as I am concerned, it's not the mistakes in your past that should define you, it's where you are right now." Titi sighed at the end of her speech. I looked at her; sometimes the girl could be so profound.

"I totally agree," I said, finally willing myself to talk. "So you made some mistakes, we all have."

"You really think so?" Mina asked, sounding so unsure. "You think people won't care?"

"No, I didn't say that O! They *will* care and you will probably be the subject of gossip for a very long time. In fact, they will be talking about you even back home in Nigeria; yes O, they will care very much." Titi had the slightest of smirks on her face, I think she was enjoying being able to stick it to Mina a little.

"What I am saying is that you should hold your head up regardless. After all you cannot change the past. There is no reason why you should become a pauper because of it."

Mina looked mortified.

"Maybe he won't even reveal it. Maybe he is bluffing," I was trying to make her feel better.

"Yeah right," Titi interjected. "I say prepare for the worst."

"And hope for the best," I countered.

Titi gave me a strange look. "Look this is not a fairytale, Amaka, this is real life."

"What's your point?"

"It is best to face the situation head on; in fact left to me I would tell people myself, that way I can control the spin."

"I can't do that," Mina said.

"You should," Titi started to reply.

Just then the phone started ringing. Mina picked it up.

"Hello?" The next thing we heard was her screaming: "STOP CALLING ME." Mina slammed down the phone. We both looked at her quizzically.

"Who was that?" Titi asked.

"Uncle Tosan. He was my mother's sugar daddy. He was also the one that took my virginity!"

Wow, the shit was really hitting the fan tonight.

Mina

Innocence

It happened one day when I was about ten. I was a fast developer, so my breasts and my hips had already started to fill out. My mother had gone to the shop leaving me alone with Uncle Tosan. He was our benefactor at this point in time, so he came and went as he pleased.

I decided to go and play with Nneka, my friend next door. I was wearing a sundress without a bra; I hated the way they felt, so whenever my mother wasn't around, I took the offending piece of clothing off. Nneka's mother eventually called me to say my mother had phoned and wanted me to go home immediately. I called her at the shop and begged to be allowed to stay and play, especially as it was only Uncle Tosan in our house. It was to no avail. She insisted I return home.

I got back home and found Uncle Tosan wearing a T shirt and shorts. He claimed he was hot even though the air conditioning was on. He was eating plantain that the maid had fried. He had sent her to the market to buy yam, because he felt like eating that as well.

I ignored him and decided to play a game on my Atari.

"Mina," he called. "Come and eat plantain with me."

"No thank you, Uncle, I am not hungry."

"Don't you know it is impolite to refuse an offer from an elder?" Uncle Tosan was big on manners. He was a British educated lawyer, from one of the affluent society families in Nigeria, and was all about being 'proper.'

"I am sorry, but I am really not hungry."

"Well then, come and sit by me then and keep me company," he said, patting the cushion next to him.

I could see that he was not going to leave me in peace so I complied.

"I remember when you were younger and you used to give me big hugs," he said smiling at me, his lips shiny from the oil from the plantain.

"You are so grown up now." Something about the look on his face made me feel uneasy. "Give me a hug now, shebi. I am still your favourite Uncle," he pleaded.

So I gave him a hug.

He put his arms around me and hugged me back. I smelt his cologne -- Polo by Ralph Lauren.

I was picturing the bottle when I felt his hands around my buttocks, squeezing them. I looked at him in alarm. He smiled.

"You like that don't you? You are just like your mother." And then he started squeezing my breasts.

Hard. He pushed himself against me on the sofa and I could feel him completely.

My heart was racing wildly. I couldn't think of what to do. No one was home; I wanted to call my mother but I couldn't get to the phone, he was too heavy. The air conditioner made too much noise for anyone to hear me if I screamed. He stood up to reposition himself and I saw that what I thought were regular shorts were actually boxer shorts.

Finally I managed to push him off me and run into my room because he was distracted by the phone ringing.

It must have been my mother. He told her we were fine and not to worry. He ended the conversation with, "Of course, I love you," and then he followed me to my room where I had fled. He tried to come in but I had locked the door.

Uncle Tosan was not to be deterred. He pushed through the door, breaking the lock. I started to scream. He grabbed my neck and told me to shut up or he would kill me. Then he threw me down on the bed. I bounced a little from the firmness of the mattress. He grabbed at me and ripped my sundress off in one motion. All I had on then were my panties. He smiled lecherously and then quickly jumped on top of me. He pushed my panties aside and entered me. I could barely breathe because of his weight on top of me. He moved quickly on top of me and the pain was excruciating. I couldn't even cry. I thought about my mother and then for a second, I wondered about my father. When he was done, he called me a good girl and said he would buy me a lot of things. I lay there quietly. My insides were hurting and the sheet was bloody.

He walked into the bathroom and I heard the faucet turn on. Then he went downstairs. I heard the maid asking him about the yam. I didn't hear his reply. Then the front door slammed.

Within seconds our maid, Tina was upstairs. She took one look at me and started to shake her head and curse in Yoruba. She pulled me to my feet and walked me to the bathroom. She made me sit on the toilet and she ran hot water into a plastic bucket. She then put me in the bathtub and proceeded to give me a bath. When she got to my legs, she kept saying "sorry O, sorry O." After the bath, she told me to lie down and then she went to make me pepper soup with yam in it.

I choked on the yam.

When my mother returned I decided I was going to tell her what Uncle Tosan had done. It was extremely hard because I didn't even really know what had happened. I stuttered through my explanation. But when I finished my mother just came closer to me and asked what I was wearing at the time.

I told her I was wearing a sundress. She asked me if I was wearing a bra and I hesitated. She slapped me hard across the cheek.

"Didn't I tell you to wear a bra?"

I started to cry. She began to berate me: "So you want to become a useless girl eh. Chasing after your own mother's boyfriend eh, my own child! See me see trouble O!"

I was shocked at my mother's response. She was blaming me! The next semester she sent me away to boarding school and she continued to see Uncle Tosan, who incidentally sent me a diamond necklace. That was when I learned that there was no such thing as love.

Titi

All that glitters

Wonders will never cease! Can you believe it? When you look at Mina, she looks like butter cannot melt in her mouth: all cool, calm and perfection. Meanwhile the chick is completely messed up. From being raped to becoming an escort, the babe has been through some shit!

It's funny, now I can understand why she is the way she is. I thought my situation was bad because my father couldn't care less about me, but Mina's is so much worse. How could her own mother choose her boyfriend over her?

Poor girl, no wonder she can be cold as winter. And now this wahala with her husband, that's definitely the last thing she needs. I tell you, you never know what is going on under people's designer clothes! Seeing the way that girl broke down can really tell you how she has been holding this all inside for years. It's a wonder it didn't destroy her. I tell you what we women go through, Na wa!

Make I no lie though, part of me feels like saying 'it serves you right!' If I tell you how many times Mina has looked down on me and basically called me a prostitute because I was honest about my background and the way I lived my life. Meanwhile Madam Etiquette was once a common escort. I tell you, when she confessed that, I was ready to start shouting. If not for Amaka's warning look, I would have had a serious laugh at her expense. The irony of life...

In fact, part of me doesn't feel sorry for her. Too bad she got raped and all that but you would think that would make her more compassionate, more approachable. Instead she became a hard bitch, always quick to tell us how smart she was by choosing a pushover for a husband and molding him to her taste. She was always talking about how to keep your man in line and all that. I guess she kept Obinna so in line that he had to break out.

I was so deep in thought about Mina that I didn't hear the phone at first. I answered it on the last ring.

It was Yinka, a cousin in Lagos and a bonafide society woman.

"Ah, Titi, is that you?" she said, laughing.

"Live and direct now! How far?"

"My dear, we dey O. You nko?"

"Ah you know me now, bodi dey for ground!"

"You know that guy you were asking me about?" Yinka asked.

"Yes now, Jeffrey Ifedike right?"

"Yes."

"Ehen, what's the gist?" I asked.

"Tell your friend to forget about him."

"Why?"

"The guy is married with three kids," she said.

I screamed. "You're not serious!"

"I am. In fact I met the wife last week, come and see her praising her hubby." Yinka went on and on about how sweet Jeffrey's wife was.

"I can't believe that guy…he even gave my friend a diamond ring," I said when I could finally get a word in.

"Don't mind them jo. He can afford it; he is a rich man so maybe a ring is nothing to him. But she should not take him seriously," Yinka insisted.

"Maybe he is planning on leaving his wife," I said.

"I doubt it; their last child is only about nine months old."

I was floored.

How was I going to tell Amaka? My people make I tell una, when it wan rain for Naija, make you forget umbrella, I hope say you get betta raincoat!

Amaka

Right on time

When I left Mina's that evening, I was so sad. How could Obinna do something like that to her? I know that things between them weren't perfect. One night at a party after he'd had a little too much to drink, he confessed to me he loved his wife but often felt he'd made a mistake by marrying her. I guess I was just foolish to think that he would work through these feelings. Now he was with someone else and Mina was left out in the cold. Should I have warned her? Or maybe the real issue is the fact that this other woman is pregnant by him. Was this all because Mina didn't seem able to have children?

Thinking about Mina not getting pregnant forced me to remember something I had been pushing to the back of my mind for some time.

My period was late.

I knew it even when Jeffrey was getting ready to leave but I put it down to stress. But by the time the baby shower came round, I knew it was a little too late to be just that so I had picked up a pregnancy test at the pharmacy. I have been carrying it around with me for days now; I guess I'm afraid to take it.

I know, in this day and age I should have been more careful. Most of the time Jeffrey and I used condoms but there were those couple of times when things were too hot and heavy for either of us to think straight and we took the chance.

One of those times I remember saying "what if" to him and he echoed it right back to me: "What if, nothing! If you get pregnant, so what? We'll have a beautiful product of our love. I love you and I will always love you. So if you get pregnant then no big deal, we want to get married anyway." After he said all that I guess I relaxed and let my guard down.

Just thinking about him made me feel warm all over. I hadn't talked to him since he had got back. It had been five days. I chalked it up to the bad phone lines in Nigeria. I only had his office number. He had explained he didn't have a phone at home and he needed to get a new GSM number anyway. I was a little surprised that he hadn't called but I felt sure he was safe. I kept trying his office line but he was always out.

When I first realized my period was late, I was a little disturbed. I was from a very conservative family. Already selling Jeffrey, a man with a child, to them, would be a little difficult. But then for me to also be pregnant would certainly cause their disapproval. At least I could be confident about how Jeffrey would feel. When I remembered what he had said that night, and how sure he was about his feelings for me, I knew that if I was pregnant, he would be happy. It would be alright as long as he was by my side.

I looked at the blue box promising results in less than a minute. I thought about how much could happen in one minute. I contemplated our life together: We would spend Saturday mornings lounging in bed, I would be cooing at the baby while Jeffrey perused the newspaper. Every couple of minutes, he would look up and be filled with love for his family and that would make him reach over and give us a kiss. At this point, little junior would be handed over to his nanny and we would make sweet languid love.

I was just about to make cloud nine when the doorbell interrupted my thoughts.

I looked through the peephole and I was a little surprised to see Titi, as she never goes anywhere unannounced. I was even more surprised to see that she came with food. She usually comes into my house and heads straight for the kitchen, chanting "Oh girl, where's the grub because your sister is hungry!"

Today she had food from the Cheesecake factory: Spicy Cashew Chicken for me and Chinese Chicken salad for her. And for dessert, two slices of German Chocolate cheesecake. I was pleasantly surprised.

"To what do I owe the honor?" I asked. "It's not my birthday or anything."

"No, it's not but you're my friend," she replied, hands on hips. "Can't a girl celebrate her friend if she wants to?"

"What's going on, Titi?" I was suspicious. I ran to the window. "Did you bash my car or something?"

"Will you stop acting crazy and come and eat this food before I eat it all!" she commanded, having dished the food onto some plates.

I obeyed and we began to eat. She was very talkative, telling me about the house she was helping Dele Thompson buy for them. She was convinced that the house was just a prelude to his proposing. She seemed to forget that just a little while ago she had been the one warning me about whirlwind romances. I had a ring to show for mine. She had nothing except a few suggestions and some sexy underwear. I kept my thoughts to myself though.

"Girl, I almost forgot. I bought your favorite champagne." Titi went into the kitchen and produced a mini bottle of Veuve Cliquot and two glasses. She popped it and poured it saying, "You know what we should drink to? Us, we should drink to us."

I started to lift the glass to my lips and then I remembered. I placed the glass down, muttering, "I'd better not."

"Why not?" Titi pounced. "Only reason I can think about not to enjoy champagne is if…" She looked at me with eyes wide.

"You're not…"

"Maybe," I said, feeling ashamed.

"Oh, Amaka." There was a piteous tone in her voice. She was silent for a few seconds. I found myself holding my breath. Suddenly her approval was very important to me.

"Oh, it's not such a big deal, Titi," I said loudly. "People get pregnant before they get married all the time these days. If I am pregnant, my parents will probably be irritated for a bit, but once we get married all will be forgiven."

She just looked at me. "Does Jeffrey know?"

"Actually he has been so busy we haven't had a chance to really talk." I said, sugarcoating the truth a bit.

"Amaka, I'm so sorry."

"No need to be," I countered. "Like I said, it's not a big deal."

"Amaka, you need to sit down. There is something I have to tell you," Titi said, shaking her head.

She looked serious, so I sat down.

Like I said, a lot can change in one minute.

Mina

New mercies

I had been holed up in my house for a couple of weeks. At first, after the whole debacle at the baby shower, I convinced myself that I could still hold my head up high. I contemplated the possible divorce settlement and figured that I would still land on my feet.

So I ventured out to the Oyeka's anniversary party, it was part of my new "be bold" strategy. I made sure I looked pristine in an Oscar de la Renta suit and my makeup was flawless. I had almost convinced myself that I was good to go, but then I walked into the house and even I could see through myself. At first they whispered, stealing glances. It took all of my resolve but I walked around the party and greeted people, even though I knew they would be talking about me and laughing beneath their smiles.

The worst were the looks of pity, the light touches on my arms, the incline of the neck and the look in their eyes that said, "sorry o, but better you than me." I felt like I was being scrubbed raw with a metal sponge. I only lasted about thirty minutes then I practically ran to my car. I was so glad that I had insisted on tinted windows, because at least I knew no one would see my tears as they burned through my foundation. After that experience I felt I could not face the world again.

My friend Chanterelle was at the party. She followed me out to my car and handed me a handkerchief to dry the tears that were welling up in my eyes. I hadn't seen her in so long but I was glad she was there that night. She didn't say a word. She just got into the car and drove me home.

The next morning I awoke to see my friend cleaning my bathroom mirror. It was sparkling. I looked in it and I was shocked at what I saw. My eyes were sunken, my hair was dirty and what's worse, a few grays were showing. I stepped on the scale and saw that I had lost almost 5 pounds. I hadn't been eating. Amaka and Titi came by every so often to check on me but they had their own lives to get back to.

Looking around I was shocked to see a thick layer of dust everywhere. With my finances gone to pieces, I had been forced to get rid of Rosa, my cleaning woman and like the rest of my life, the house was now a mess.

Chanterelle finally spoke up. "Mmhmm, it's a mess alright," she said, following my line of vision. "Girl, we've got to clean this place up and then, we'll get to work on you."

She handed me a bucket and a cloth. I looked at her looking at me.

"Now listen," she said, "what are you going to do, curl up and just die? Women have been through worse and survived. Take that bucket and get to work. A clean house allows for clear thought."

She was right. I took the bucket and started scrubbing the bath tub. As I scrubbed I thought about my mother. Every day of her life, people had gossiped about her.

I remember once being out with her when all of a sudden a woman had walked up and poured dirty water on her. She was soaked top to bottom and this woman had stood there, calling her an ashewo, a prostitute. Even though a crowd had started to gather, my mother calmly pulled out her handkerchief from her bag and wiped her face and then she just walked away, making the screaming woman look like the crazy one. I felt proud that day. Even though I was old enough to know that what the woman said was a sort of truth, she had shown me what became a cardinal rule for me: a true lady never ever shows her true emotions.

Chanterelle pulled me out of my musing by calling my name. I looked up to see her sitting on top of the toilet seat.

"Look, Mina, you are my friend and I have to tell you the truth. For years you have treated the people that love you like crap, especially your husband. You have taken the wonderful life God gave you and screwed it up."

Was she for real, I thought. "Is this your idea of being supportive?" I asked her.

"Yes," she said. "Maybe if I had been straight up with you before, you might have changed your ways and still have your husband."

I felt like slapping her. "Who are you to judge me?" I demanded. "You don't live my life."

"No, but I am your friend and I have to tell you that now is the time to change your life, time to change your ways."

I walked into the bedroom and grabbed her handbag and shoes. I placed them on the floor in front of her.

"You know what, Chanterelle? You can leave. Thanks, but no thanks."

"Mina, stop sticking your head in the sand. You have to get up and face your life. Obinna is divorcing you and you have to get it together."

"You think I don't know that my husband is leaving me?" I shouted. "You think you have to tell me that my life is falling apart."

Chanterelle just stood there looking sadly at me. "I'm sorry, Mina, I'm just trying to help."

"Keep your help," I said. I walked her to the door to show that I really wanted her to leave.

When we got there, she stopped and stood. I thought she was waiting for me to open the door so I reached for the handle. She grabbed my hand and turned to face me.

"Mina, I'm really sorry. I haven't handled this very well and there is something I should have done since the day you told me about your husband's affair."

I thought she was talking about the way I had dealt with Carolina so I finally conceded, "No, you were right. I shouldn't have confronted that woman."

"I am not talking about that," she said. "Mina, something has happened to me. I have become a Christian and ever since I accepted Christ, I have found that I prefer to live my life a different way. I'm sorry that I came across as judging you; I didn't mean to sound that way. You are a wonderful person and I just wish I could find a better way to express myself. That day you called, instead of offering advice, I should have prayed with you," she said.

I was surprised at her. What was she talking about prayer for? Was prayer going to get me back my husband? Was it going to erase the humiliation I felt? When I voiced my feelings, she said yes. Prayer could do all of those things. I looked at her more closely. She looked the same: same incredible sense of style, same biting wit, same no nonsense attitude. How did she become a "Jesus freak"?

"Look Mina, I unfortunately don't have the time now to share my story with you but suffice it to say, my experience has been life changing. Now is the time for you to consider changing your life. I know you must be going through a lot right now and I can't really change today's circumstances but if you will allow me to pray with you, I feel sure God in his mercy will answer."

I was ambivalent about her praying but because she had been there for me when I needed her, and this was something she clearly felt wanted to do, I let her go ahead.

At first when she started praying, I let my mind wander but then she started talking about healing my spirit and the hurt that I carried inside. It was as if she had been there when I told Titi and Amaka about the rape. She couldn't have known but yet she was praying for exactly what I needed.

When she started asking God to make me whole and help me understand that I too am worthy of love, I felt tears roll down my cheeks. I thought about my father -- the famous Chief Amakiri George. All my life, I had dreamed of him one day recognizing me as his daughter. I always thought that he had never claimed my mother and me because we weren't good enough; I wasn't good enough. He had several children by his wife and even some by other women that he not only claimed but reveled in, yet never me. I even tried contacting him a few times when I was young but nothing.

By the end of the prayer I was sobbing as Chanterelle held me. She wiped my tears when she was done and said, "Mina, I would love it if you would come to my church on Sunday."

I nodded my head in submission.

After Chanterelle left, I started to feel renewed. I walked back into the room and looked in my purse for a card that Titi had given me. Eli Stein -- he was supposed to be a great divorce lawyer. I called him and made an appointment. And then I walked into my bathroom, took a hot shower and washed my hair.

I was feeling pretty good about myself so I decided to go down to the Farmers' Market. I love it there. Filled with exotic organic fruit and vegetables, an assortment of meats and seafood and beautiful fresh flowers, it is a peaceful place for me whenever I am stressed.

I picked up some beautiful ginger flowers and birds of paradise, and added a few other striking blooms to create a beautiful centerpiece. As I walked towards the cashier's desk, two different women stopped me and asked if they had more arrangements like that on display. When I told them that I had arranged it myself they were very impressed and asked me if I had a card or something. I laughed and momentarily forgot my situation as I responded, "Oh no, I don't work for a living!"

As I drove up to the house, I noticed that the flowers had started to bloom in the garden. I loved my garden. I got out of the car and looked it over, thinking about how the landscape architect I had hired had really captured my intentions. The roses and zinnias and hydrangeas were all strategically placed to set off the beauty of the flagstone driveway and the brick of the house.

I was going to miss this house.

Inside I placed my arrangement on the foyer table, where it would get the most light and usually be seen by all. I looked around the filthy house, dust and dirt everywhere, and realized I had never actually cleaned it myself. I went upstairs and changed into a pair of jeans and an old college t-shirt. In the washroom I dug out the cleaning items that Rosa always used, and then I got down to the task at hand.

An hour later I had not even completed the kitchen. My hands were red and I was sweaty and tired, but my mind was alert. It was as if I had been spring-cleaning my brain too.

I thought again about my mother and the cardinal rule I had learned from her, to never show my hurt. But really, who was fooling whom? When I told stories about my mother, or thought about her, it was often in those moments when she had been stoic and graceful. How many times did I see her demean herself before men? Begging and crying just for a little more cash. I never thought about those times, and I certainly never spoke about them to anyone else.

I thought about myself and tried to make an honest assessment. I had become a bitch. In every sense of the word! I had always been horrible to Obinna and of course, like a cliché, it was only after he was gone that I had started to appreciate him. I had so carefully made a disaster of my life. In fact I had screwed up, pure and simple. As I continued to clean, I started to cry and I cried and cried as I cleaned and cleaned. Somehow with all the hard work, I started to feel better.

By evening I had finished the house; every room was vacuumed, every tile was gleaming. My body was sore and I was spent but I also felt good and proud, like I had at least accomplished something. I got into the tub and soaked. I looked at the Venetian tile that I had picked out and had shipped from Italy and it was as if I was seeing it for the first time. It was quite ugly. Obinna never liked it, but I had seen it in House and Garden magazine and I had to have the best, or so I thought. I took a deep breath and then I had a thought. I would simply change the tile. I would get something pedestrian from Home Depot or Lowes. I would fix it.

I got out of the tub with an idea. I would fix everything. I had been too arrogant. Too proud. I would fix it. I would call Obinna and tell him I loved him. No, I would go over there and tell him. That's all he really wanted to hear. I had been too aloof. I would show him that I could humble myself.

I got dressed and put on a little make up. I thought I looked quite pretty, in my silk Diane von Furstenberg wrap dress with Louboutin stilettos. Then I remembered the tile. So overdone it was ugly. I needed to show Obinna something different. So I put on a pair of jeans and a polo shirt and then some sneakers. I looked strange to myself but it had to be done. I pulled my hair back into a ponytail. Then I grabbed my keys and drove over to his condo.

I pulled up to the apartment building and walked up the first flight of stairs. I was a little anxious. What would I do if Carolina answered the door? What kind of situation was I setting myself up for? It was the kind of thing that I advised my friends to never do. Once you beg to a man, you lose power. I sighed, who was I kidding? I had no power left to lose. I had to get him back whatever it took; I had worked too hard and too long.

I took a deep breath and started to knock on the door. It opened almost immediately. I was suddenly face to face with Obinna, who was dressed in tack pants and a t-shirt. He was carrying a trash bag, he was apparently on his way to throwing it out. He looked shocked to see me.

"Mina! What are you doing here?" he exclaimed. Then he must have thought I came to cause a scene, because he started guarding the front door with his body. It smarted to know he was trying to protect her from me. I was dumbstruck with pain.

"Mina!" he said forcefully, "What do you want?"

"Obinna, I just…wanted to talk for a moment," I said, my voice wavering slightly.

His face softened. "Are you ok?" he asked.

"As well as can be expected," I responded.

"Ok, well talk," he said.

I heard a rustling at the door. The little witch was probably eavesdropping. I had to proceed anyway. This was a drastic situation.

"Obinna, I want you back, I didn't treat you as well as I should have and I understand why you did what you did. I am prepared to accept your child but I want us to work on our marriage. We had too much to throw away," I said in a quick rush.

He was quiet for a moment. Then he looked at me. "Mina, I really loved you, but being with you was too hard. It was always do this or that. I was never quite good enough and quite frankly I am tired of all that. I just want peace. Truth be told I still have a lot of feelings for you, I love you; but in this case, love is not enough.

"How can you say that, Obinna," I said, as tears began to well in my eyes.

"Mina, I'm sorry but it's the truth."

"So after all that I have done for you, after everything…"

"I knew it!" He shouted, cutting me off. "You haven't changed one bit. What have you done for me? What?!! I made you! You used me as a way to get ahead, you thought I was your personal piece of clay that you could mould into whatever you want, but I am a man and I have had enough. I worked my ass off to get where I am today. Have you ever passed one medical exam? Did you kill yourself working all night and all day during residency? You did nothing!" he roared.

I was shocked. My eyes were wide and dry eyed suddenly. I finally understood how bad things were between us. I had no idea he felt this strongly.

"Mina, I think you better leave now," he said as he picked up the bag of trash that he had put down during his tirade. He started to walk past me.

I reached out to touch his arm. "Obinna, wait!" I said.

He pushed my arm off forcefully. "Don't touch me. Understand this, it is over. I don't want to be with a woman who is so full of herself. I care for Carolina and I will make a life with her and this baby."

I started to sob.

Obinna sighed, "Mina, just go home. Go find yourself another rich man!" he said and then he walked away, never once looking back.

I heard the rustling behind the door again. She was probably laughing at me. I had become a laughing stock to everyone. I felt so humiliated. I ran to my car and let the tears fall.

After a while, I composed myself enough to drive. I don't know how I made it home because I drove like a maniac. I was speeding down the highway even though I couldn't really see through my tears. I was sick of my life, why was everything going wrong? I wondered what would happen if I just took my hands off the wheel. What more did I have to lose anyway?

I had the radio on but I wasn't paying attention. A popular song had been playing and then the inspirational supplement came on -- a Christian spot, played by a morning DJ:

"Every life is worth living. As far as you have breath, you have an opportunity to change your life. No matter how low you feel, no matter how messed up you are, you are wonderful in God's eyes"

Not me, I thought. *I am a complete mess. I can't even keep my marriage together.*

"...He created you; He took his time to make you perfectly. Even if you have made a mess of your life, I'm telling you it's not too late to change your life. Don't throw in the towel. You can change your life, if you would just give it a try."

I changed the station. I couldn't listen to this; I scanned for some music but the words kept repeating in my head. How could I change my life when everything was falling apart around me? I was lost in my thoughts when I realized I was pulling into my driveway.

I went to my bathroom and ran hot water for a bath. All I wanted to do was soak in the tub and get away from the world. I took off my clothes and stepped into the steaming, sweetly scented water. I leaned my head back and started to think. Somehow I had really destroyed my life. How did this happen? I lay there for a while just thinking.

I must have fallen asleep because I woke up with a start. The water had turned cold. I stood up and toweled off. As I dried my skin, I thought about my marriage. Obinna was right; I had been manipulative and controlling. I had never loved him. I began to admit to myself that I had driven Obinna into the arms of another woman. I had put him through so much. I had never seen him as a man, much less a good one. Instead I had put my worth in money and material things.

I thought then that what I needed to do was to begin to forgive myself. I started to forgive myself for messing up, for being a bitch on more than one occasion.

There were other people I knew I needed to forgive. My mother first. I thought about everything she had put me through. I became who I was because of her, but I could see that actually she hadn't known any better. I resolved to let go of my anger towards her.

Then there was my father and men in general, and even Uncle Tosan for whom I had carried so much hatred for all these years. It would be hard but I made up my mind to try and forgive them all too.

I finally started to feel something else besides sadness; I started to feel hopeful.

I walked into the room and looked in the mirror. Who was I? I would no longer be a wife. I pulled my hair out of the ponytail and shook it loose; it was time for a change. I was ready to change, but how?

I thought perhaps I should pray. I hadn't prayed in such a long time that I wasn't quite sure how to begin. I couldn't even remember the Our Father prayer from my confirmation classes. I thought I should use a Bible but then after searching for a few minutes, realized that I probably didn't have one in the house.

So instead I simply knelt by the foot of my empty bed and I began:

"Dear God, it's been so long since I have prayed that I don't really know what to say. I want to tell you that I am sorry. Sorry for being the way I was; well, sorry for everything.

My grandmother when she was alive used to tell me you had a plan for all of us and I don't know what your plan is for me, but I am ready for it.

My marriage has fallen apart and I am not going to ask you to heal it because I know now that I was selfish in that marriage and Obinna could never have been happy. He seems to be happy with this woman. Help me to wish them well.

I don't know what I am going to do, but please give me the strength to get through it.

I stayed there for a long time, with wet eyes and a broken heart and then before I knew it, the sun was beginning to shine through my window and I looked at the clock and it was 5:30 am. Suddenly I knew what I was going to do. My grandmother, who I saw very little of, but who I thought about a lot these days, used to tell me something: "Is there any solace that cannot be found?" As I thought about her, I knew that doing this would make me feel better and it might even change my life.

I would go to Chanterelle's church.

Titi

Send down the rain

Oh boy, when it rains, it pours. First Mina loses her husband and now Amaka might be pregnant by a man who is married and didn't even have the decency to tell her.

When I broke the news to her she was devastated. She kept asking me if I was sure. I told her absolutely. I wouldn't have told her if I wasn't sure. She vacillated between anger and anguish, cursing out the bastard and then declaring her love for him. She was completely undone. Add to that the possibility of being pregnant, it was just crazy.

I was so through with that Jeffrey that if I ran into him today he would have a serious problem. Imagine declaring his love like that and having no real intentions. Poor Maksy!

That's why I appreciated men like Dele Thompson, men who came without a whole lot of sentimental nonsense. He told it like it was. I knew he liked me and now, with his impending proposal, he had probably seen that not only did we connect physically and mentally, I would be a fantastic asset to his life.

I was supposed to be meeting Dele at the estate. We were to see the realtor to sign more documents and also the interior decorator to discuss customizing the house.

As I pulled up to the office, I saw Dele's black Mercedes S600. I parked and did a quick check in my mirror. Hair: check. Gloss: just right. Cleavage: well just perfect. I smoothed down my skirt. I was very excited in every way; I wasn't wearing panties because I planned to surprise Dele later on.

I walked into the realtor's office with a breezy, "Hi Bob," and I was just about to plant a kiss on Dele's lips when I noticed another woman sitting next to him.

She was petite and refined in a St John's suit and pearls.

"Hello, Titi," Dele said. "Titi is my realtor. She is fantastic, which is why she is getting this amazing commission." Dele explained all this to the woman while looking directly at me, a hard expression on his face.

"Titi, this is my fiancée, Karen Omoruyi."

"How do you do?" Karen had a clipped British accent. She extended her hand limply.

"Thank you so much for looking after Dele and helping us find this house. I was too busy in London to come down any sooner." She smiled as she asked, "I hope we will see you at the wedding?"

I was floored. I sat down quickly to disguise my wobbly knees. I looked over at Bob who had seen Dele and I canoodling in the past. He was no doubt titillated at the chance to watch this drama unfold. Seeing his sly smirk, I collected myself. Dele I could deal with later, but we were talking about a hundred thousand dollar commission here. So I became the professional as always.

"I would love to attend," I politely replied to Karen.

As Dele and Karen signed the papers, I snuck a glance at her ring. It was quite exquisite. It was a pear shaped stone, at least three carat, flanked by smaller diamonds on each side. The stone was set in platinum. I had to fight back tears.

Suddenly Dele went outside to take a phone call and Bob excused himself, which left Karen and I alone together.

I was debating whether to tell her that her soon-to-be husband had been doing more that look for houses with me, when she leaned towards me with a cold look on her face.

"Don't think that I am not aware of the fact that you have been more than his realtor. I know Dele; he has a penchant for loose women. I don't care because whores like you make it easier for me, you see I don't have to do the degrading things you do, but then again, I don't get paid for my services.

"Now listen to me very carefully. I fully intend to live life as Mrs. Dele Thompson, so while you may have fucked him in the past, just be aware that *I* will be his wife soon. He will always treat me like a queen and you will always be just his whore, so enjoy whatever little perks you have already gotten and your cheap little g-strings because that is all you will get from this man because you are nothing to him but a cheap hole for him to stick!"

Just as she finished speaking, Dele and Bob both walked in. Karen switched gears like a pro: "Dele darling, I think we can let Titi go. After all we don't need her help in choosing the cabinet wood for goodness sake, and the poor dear looks tired."

Dele was only too happy to agree. "Bob, all is in order for Titi to get her commission right?" he asked.

Bob nodded and I murmured some parting words and then I practically ran out of the office.

I had never been so humiliated in my life.

Amaka

The truth will set you free

Honestly I couldn't believe what Titi had told me. Jeffrey had spoken of his love for me so sincerely and I had never pressed him to do so.

I had to call him to find out what was going on. My hand shook as I dialed the number to his office in Lagos.

I listened to the double ring and thought of my parents at home. What would they think if they knew their only daughter was involved with a married man? Everything I had tried to avoid had come to be. I had brought shame to their name.

Surprisingly, I heard Jeffrey's characteristic drawl on the line.

"Jeffrey?"

"Amaka? Is that you?" Jeffrey said, sounding excited.

"Yes, it is." I was too unsure of myself to say more at this moment.

"Baby, I have missed you."

"Really?" In spite of myself, my heart was beginning to race.

"Of course, I have. Why do you sound like this?" He was starting to sound a little unsure of himself.

I blurted it out, "Jeffrey, how many children do you have?"

"Amaka, are you alright? What kind of question is that?"

"Don't stall, just answer the question. Better still, I'll answer it for you. Does the number three sound about right?" My anger was rising now, threatening to explode.

He started to reply, but then he fell silent.

"Oh, you have nothing to say? You bastard...Why couldn't you just tell me the truth? Why?!" I started screaming.

Jeffrey's voice was soft now. "Amaka, calm down, it's not what you think."

"It's not what I think? Which part? The part about you having a wife or your last baby being nine months old?"

He gasped when he realized just how much I knew and I could hear the wheels turning in his head, thinking about how to get out of it.

"You goddamn liar! Why did you tell me all those things? Why did you say you loved me and give me a ring?" I continued screaming.

"Amaka, I am sorry," he said quietly.

"Yes, you are, you bastard; yes you are! Here I was thinking you were a good man, and you are not even a man at all."

"Amaka, I didn't mean to hurt you," he jumped in. "Everything I said to you was true. I fell in love with you. It's true, at first when I saw you it was just about sex. You were the sexiest woman I had ever seen. But then as we got to know each other, I began to feel alive, more alive than I had ever felt in my life, and you did that for me!"

I was quiet and when Jeffrey heard I wasn't going to respond or yell any more, he continued pleading his case, now sounding a little bolder.

"I really do love you. I honestly contemplated a life with you; I didn't want to come back to Lagos."

"So where does the lie end and the truth begin, Jeffrey?" I asked, suddenly feeling exhausted and spent.

"I did have a daughter out of wedlock, but the truth was that I succumbed to family pressure and we got married by the time she was a month old. It was the biggest mistake of my life."

"Jeffrey, I may be many things but stupid is not one of them. You don't continue having children with someone you don't love on some level."

"Amaka, I know you are not stupid, but you don't understand. After a while I just gave up; I guess I just decided to go along with the marriage. I stopped believing in the possibility of feeling like I do about you."

As he spoke, I began to allow myself to feel and hope. Even though I knew it was all probably bullshit, I let myself go back to that place where all that was between us was romance, kisses and a world of promise.

"Amaka," he called my name softly. "I made a mistake, I should have told you. I really don't want to lose you."

I shook my head and with my hand on my stomach, without a word, I replaced the phone on the receiver.

I looked at myself in the mirror. How did this happen? I thought only bad girls had relationships with married men. How did I allow myself to become part of that group? I searched my face for changes. Did my eyes have a more knowing look, did they belie my innocence?

I looked down at my stomach. Placed my hand low on the spot that should have been cramping close to a month ago and went to the bathroom to do what I should have done weeks ago.

I took the test.

When I saw the plus sign, I just sat on the toilet and thought about my life and the life growing inside of me.

How could love go so horribly wrong?

Mina

In the church house

"Brethren, I want to tell you something deep right now. It's never too late. As long as you have breath, it is never too late. Now I don't care what you've been through, I don't even care what you have put people through, it's not too late right now to come back home."

I listened to the preacher call people forward to give their lives to Christ and I felt a tugging in my spirit but I forced myself to remain still. Rigid. I wasn't going to go forward. I just came for a bit of solace; a sense of direction.

"Right now is the time to change your life. I know how you feel; you might be so sick of what you see in the mirror, because while the world sees that suit and tie, that perfectly made up face, you see someone who is dejected, who has been rejected and you think you can never be any better."

I felt a tear roll down my eye. Then another one followed. I tried to hide it with my hair.

"You see, my God is the God of second chances. He loves you just as you are. Right as you are, even in the midst of your stinking mess. All He wants to do is help you get clean again. Won't you come, brother; won't you come, sister?"

I felt as if the whole church was staring at me. My tears had started to flow in earnest now and I couldn't stop them. I knew I needed something but I didn't want to become one of those Jesus people. You know, 'always too blessed to be stressed' and all that. I was a realist. Yes, I had gotten myself into a crazy situation but I could get myself together, all I needed was a good cry and I had already had it.

"I know you think you can do it by yourself; I know you think you aren't ready to be weak. Sister, I want to tell you, if you allow yourself to be weak then He will make you strong. Acknowledge that you are broken and He will make you whole. You will be whole again. Whole from that rape, from that molestation, whole from that mistake, whole from that abortion, whole from that hurt that's eating you alive. Come on and lay your burden down and let Jesus come into your life."

I was talking myself into leaving when I realized I was walking towards the altar.

"Come on, sister; God loves you."

I was so scared and so ashamed.

"I know your fears, but He wants me to tell you that He loves you and He has a plan for you."

I kept my eyes down, and I noticed that my white blouse had become stained with the mixture of tears and foundation.

"All of Heaven is rejoicing, sister."

Finally I reached the altar and I was so spent already that I stumbled and almost fell. The preacher reached out to steady me. Suddenly I felt safe and warm again.

I looked up and he had his hands over mine.

"Let us pray," he said softly as the choir started singing *"I Surrender"*.

I don't remember what the preacher said but at the time it was just what I needed to hear, and when I replied "Amen", I meant it. It seemed like something changed inside me. When I walked out of the New Mercies Tabernacle that morning, I felt like a new person.

I finally felt strong enough to do something that I should have done years ago. I decided to confront my mum. Since that day that Uncle Tosan had hurt me, she had never again spoken of it. In fact, she had acted like I should be grateful to Uncle Tosan for allowing me to hang around them.

But after my mother had dismissed and blamed me, and later sent me away to boarding school, I had been broken. Like a precious and fragile heirloom, I had thought I could never be put back together again. All the warmth went out of me, all the emotion and all the passion, like the blood from a slaughtered goat. She had hurt me. In fact, she had damaged me, destroyed all that was sweet and loving within me. I had to reclaim myself and the only way I could do that was to confront her, my mother.

Titi

Devastation

I pulled into the parking lot of my condominium building and just sat in my car thinking. I turned off the ignition, deliberately sitting in the heat.

I had been such a fool. As I cried hot angry tears, I thought about my life. Why did I always set myself up like this? All I had been to Dele was his 'anytime he wanted me' delight. My God! Yes, I talked a good game about being sexually liberated and all that but through it all, I still wanted someone to want me; someone to see me as more than just tits and ass.

I couldn't believe I had let that jackass and his bitch hurt me like this. I shook my head and then thought I had only myself to blame. I had degraded myself, made myself into a purely sexual toy for him. Why did I still have this sugar daddy mentality even after all these years? I mean I could take care of myself now. Why was I still chasing after these rich men? Was it worth it, when most of them are assholes anyway?

Suddenly everything seemed so clear. So clear that I don't know why it took me so long to get there. I knew, finally and deeply, that I didn't need this shit. I didn't need these men. I was going to focus on myself from now on.

In the heat of the car, I could feel sweat trickling to the small of my back; I decided then that I was going to make things happen for myself from now on. I decided to open up my own real estate firm and to look into some serious real estate investing.

When I finally got out of the car, the back of my suit was damp but my mind was clear. I walked to the elevator and as the numbers lit up, I felt like finally things were looking up.

I walked into my condo and threw my keys on the coffee table. I felt like cooking a meal for myself so I walked into the kitchen and put a saucepan on the stove. Even though I didn't usually cook, Amaka and Mina had made sure I had solid cookware. The saucepan was cast iron and heavy. Just as I looked in the fridge to see what I could throw together, thinking that I didn't have much to go with, I felt a sharp pain around my neck.

"So you have been fucking around eh?"

It was Segun. And he was squeezing my neck tightly. He screamed, "What did I tell you bitch?"

I gasped for air.

"I told you that if I ever found out you had been with another man, I would kill you."

I knew he meant it. I had to do something or he would kill me. Dele was one kind of problem but Segun was a mad man. I had to get him out of my life for good.

"You are such a useless bitch! I made you! When I met you, you had nothing! You weren't even a good fuck!" He squeezed harder.

"I am going to kill you today and no one is going to care."

I was gasping for air and then I saw the saucepan. As he continued his tirade, I tried to reach for it without him noticing. My fingers were almost on it when Segun saw what I was doing. He knocked me down to the floor.

"Ah, you want to fight me?"

I fell to the floor, holding my throat and taking precious gulps of air. My mind started racing. "Jesus, help me," I prayed as I struggled.

He looked at me on the floor with a menacing look in his eyes. I tried to get up but he kicked me in the stomach and I could taste blood and bile. He kicked my head and the room began to spin, I started to fade into oblivion when I heard a thud.

I woke up to see Emmanuel there with a washcloth dabbing at my face. Segun was down on the floor and the saucepan next to him.

"I have called the police," Emmanuel said quietly.

For some strange reason, I didn't want him to see me like this. I tried to move and was rewarded by searing pain.

"Don't," he instructed, still dabbing at my face. "You are safe now."

Mina

If God is for me

I listened to the sound of the ringing phone, preparing myself for my conversation with my mother. My heart was thumping inside of me because, quite frankly, I was scared. I don't know why but my mother had always intimidated me. Physically she is quite petite but there is something about her, a malevolent spirit that is frightening. When I was a little girl, she would pinch me for no reason at all and when I cried out in pain, she would smile and say, "You better get used to it, life is nothing but pain."

When she picked up the phone, I could hear the wind in the background. She was in the car.

"Hello, Mummy."

She began shouting at me at once. "What is this I have heard? You have allowed one local girl to come and snatch your husband?"

"Well, Mummy," I started to explain.

"You are so stupid! After all these years, you still haven't learnt anything. You couldn't even secure a docile man like Obinna. You are a disgrace to me!"

"Mummy, the situation is complicated," I said softly in my own defense. I was near tears already.

"What is complicated? It looks simple to me. You have been removed from your husband's house and you have nothing, no career to stand on, nothing. Well, I hope you have some savings or something, because if you are expecting even a penny from me, you will be sorely disappointed. I have my own needs to meet." She interrupted her tirade to give the driver directions on where he should turn.

"I told you that you should have seen Tosan when he was in the US; he would have been able to help you."

The mention of Uncle Tosan stirred something inside me. "You know what, Mummy. I don't expect anything from you, not money, not help and certainly not a loving gesture," I said. "You are calling me a disgrace? It is you that is the disgrace; for God's sake even a rat knows how to love its children better than you. How dare you mention Uncle Tosan to me? That pedophile!

"And as for you, may God forgive you for peddling your only child for the price of some trinkets and Vuitton. Is that what I am worth? Is that what you are worth? Well, let me tell you something. You may have been the vessel that brought me into the world, but you have never given me life. Instead you have tried everything possible to take it. You think I am foolish?

You are right! I am foolish for ever listening to you, foolish for ever allowing you to influence my life. Well, let me announce one thing to you, I am done!" I finally drew a breath.

My mother was silent. For a second, I thought she had hung up on me, but then I heard the faint cry of a street peddler, shouting how cold his ice water was.

I started to speak a little softer.

"Mummy, I don't know why you are the way you are, but you were never there for me. Mummy, Uncle Tosan raped me. Your boyfriend raped me and you sanctioned it. You sent me away to boarding school and continued cavorting with a man who didn't think enough of you or your own blood.

"You talk about being so wise, but you forget that I have always been there. I was there when we were thrown out of our home by thugs because your boyfriend's wife had found out he was paying for our apartment.

"I was there when another boyfriend beat you so badly you had to sleep in the hospital. I was there when women spat on you and called you ashewo to your face! Between me and you, who is the foolish one? Believe me, I know I have made my mistakes with Obinna, but I will never follow the path you have taken. Today I am reclaiming myself. I am choosing to mother myself."

"Mina," my mother finally spoke.

I held my breath, thinking that maybe my words had affected her somehow.

"Mina," she repeated coldly, "if this is all you have to say to me, then don't call me ever again." She hung up on me.

I listened to the beeping sound for a long time but by the time I heard the automated voice ask if I'd like to make another call, I realized that I was not devastated. I was alright. In fact, I was relieved. I had told her what I had to say, her response was not important. I had unburdened myself and I could finally begin to move forward.

Amaka

The truth will set you free -- Part 2

All last night I was thinking about what to do. I couldn't accept the fact that Jeffrey was married. Maybe it was as he had said. He wasn't happy. Maybe he was really my soul mate. Maybe this would be my only real chance at love. How could I just let it go like that? Surely what we felt for each other couldn't be false?

Ever since I had called Jeffrey, he had been calling me, sending emails, trying to contact me. I had to believe that what we shared was real.

I decided that since we had a child to think about, I would try and make things work with him. Maybe he would leave his wife. I didn't quite know what he would do, but I knew he loved me and if he did, he would love this life inside of me.

I decided to call him to say all this, to tell him about our baby.

He was in the office even though it was past 9 pm in Lagos. He answered on the first ring.

"Hello," he said.

"It's me."

"I knew you'd call, that's why I waited."

"Jeffrey?"

"Yes?" I could hear him holding his breath.

"Do you really love me?" I asked.

He exhaled. "Yes, Amaka, I meant everything I said to you. It's just that my life is complicated. I want you in my life. I need you in my life. I have been like a crazy person since I last talked to you," he continued. "Please, whatever you do, don't walk away from me."

"Jeffrey, what are you saying? How can I be in your life if you are married? Are you suggesting I be your mistress?" I asked with my voice barely above a whisper.

He exhaled and then he said, "Mistress…no that sounds so sordid. You are my soul mate, the one with whom my heart lays. Just give me some time to figure this out."

"Jeffrey, tell me honestly, do you really mean what you are saying now?" I pleaded. "I really need you to be open with me; after all you have nothing more to lose."

"Amaka, I don't know how to convince you, you are the love of my life. I am so sorry I didn't tell you earlier about my situation, but it doesn't change how I feel about you. I just need some time to sort out my situation." He sounded so earnest.

"Well, I can give you about nine months," I finally said.

"What?" Jeffrey paused. "What's that supposed to mean?"

"I mean nine months, Jeffrey. I am pregnant."

His tone switched instantly. "How is that possible?" he demanded.

"What do you mean? You were there!" I replied.

"But we always used protection," he insisted

"Not always," I responded.

Jeffrey fell silent.

"So what are you going to do?" he finally asked, his voice sounding tight.

"What am I going to do, don't you mean we?"

"Amaka, I already have my children," he said

Did he just say 'my children'?

"I don't want to have that kind of life with you."

I was shocked into silence.

Jeffrey went on, "I mean, what we have is beautiful. It's more than the typical mom and dad, husband and wife thing. It transcends that, that's so ordinary, that's what I already have with my wife. With you, I have a second chance at a pleasurable life and I don't want to ruin it."

"Ruin it, with our child?" I cried in disbelief.

"Don't say it like that," he said quietly.

"How should I say it then?"

He took a deep breath. "Amaka, I want to be with you, but I don't want you with a child."

When I heard him say that, it was as if I was really hearing him for the first time. I don't even remember what came after that, all I could wonder was how I could have thought this narcissistic jerk was my soul mate? The only soul mate he had was himself. All he wanted was what he wanted, when he wanted it. I was a fool to think any different.

All the emotion I felt for him drained out of me. It was obvious to me now that what he claimed to feel for me was nothing more than a passing fancy. I was not his soul mate, not a partner, just a girl he had shagged sometime. I thought back on all our conversations and what I had thought then was a deep but easy connection between us began to look more and more like forced charm. Everything I had thought was an indication of his love for me began to look like pure game. He probably had it down to an art.

I didn't want the relationship anymore, but I still had this last tie to him, our child.

I needed to really think about what to do. I wasn't ready to become a single mother and I couldn't bear to think about my parents' reaction. They would be so disappointed.

It seemed like I had only one option.

I could just hear my mother's voice filled with disappointment. "You have brought shame onto my head O," she would wail. "My people, tell me what I did wrong eh? Instead of marrying a decent man, you want to go a have a baby for a married man, like a common prostitute! Ha, my enemies they want to kill me!"

I cringed as I imagined this, but I wept when I pictured my father's face. I knew him, he would not fuss and yell, he would tell me that he was my father and he would support me in any way he could. But his face would be lined with disappointment and he would be stooped over with worry.

I looked at myself in the mirror. I barely recognized myself as tears ran down my face. I had really lost myself. What had I done? I had compromised myself so much; now I had made a terrible mistake. I had never imagined I would be in this position. I was never promiscuous; counting Jeffrey I had only slept with a total of three men in my entire adult life. I was not the sort of woman who could visit the abortion clinic like it was nothing. At that moment I saw my own judgment in my reflection. I was those women and they were me. Who is to say what they were feeling or going through? Who was to judge? Father, forgive me…

The rest of the week went by in a blur of nothingness. I went through the motions like a character from *The Matrix*. I dulled the pain at night with tranquilizers and chugged coffee all day to remain perky. I made an appointment at Planned Parenthood, still vacillating between keeping the baby or not.

But though I was in private turmoil, I was amazed at my ability to carry on everyday life. I smiled at the neighbors, made small talk with the lady at the bookshop, even entertained a come-on or two. All the while there was a debate raging in my head and in my heart. It was so weird. I would be buying a cup of coffee at Starbucks and the girl would ask me if I wanted whipped cream. Almost immediately my mind would be filled with visions of babies floating on fat, white, marshmallow-like clouds and while I was watching them, I would hear my voice say, "yes, whipped cream." The words came out of my mouth from a different part of my brain.

By the week's end, I was a basket case. I had cancelled on girls' night, which of course prompted visits from Titi first, and Mina later.

They were both angels.

Titi sat me down and gave me some hard truths. "Maksy, I love you, but you can't continue doing this. You need to make a decision and whatever you choose, I am with you a hundred percent. Stop beating yourself up about making a mistake. Stop worrying about what your parents will think. Think about yourself and if you are ready to be a mother. You are not taking care of yourself either way; and my friend, I am not going to stand by while you fall into a depression."

I was amazed. Here was this woman who had been through her own drama reaching out to me, I was so moved that by the time Mina showed me her own level of love, I knew I was going to be okay.

Mina

A new creation

I never thought I would say this but I am blessed.

After I confronted my mother, I decided to call Obinna. It was a hard conversation for me but I felt it was necessary. He was expecting me to rant and rave and rain curses on him, so he was wholly unprepared for what I said.

I apologized. For everything!

I told him how I always thought that by choosing a man like him, I could make my life perfect finally but all I had succeeded in doing was almost ruining his. I told him that I didn't want a messy divorce and that I wouldn't stand in the way of his happiness. Even I could see that Carolina was good for him.

By the time I finished talking I was in tears, and he was moved for the first time in a long while. He spoke to me about when we first met and how he had been so wowed by me. He told me I was indeed very special and how glad he was that I had finally changed for the better.

He apologized also for hurting me, and assured me that I would get my fair due in the divorce. He didn't have any desire to live as lavishly as we had been doing and neither did Carolina so he was prepared to be generous. When we ended the conversation, he told me that he had really loved me and probably always would.

I felt teary for a little while afterwards but I didn't cry. I had made so many mistakes in my life but I knew that my life was not over.

It felt like I was coming out of a cocoon.

I drove over to Titi's house to see her. She had been through a horrible ordeal with that thug, Segun. Thankfully he is out of her life for good. The police arrested him and apparently he was wanted for the murder of some man down in Mississippi and had some other charges against him. It sounds like he will be gone for a long time.

Plus, this guy Emmanuel has been hanging around her ever since, checking in on her, taking care of little things for her. I could tell that he is really into her, even though he is not the sort to say it outright. I hoped Titi would give him a chance; he may not be rich but he has a calm, sweet spirit around him.

After I left Titi's, I went over to see Amaka. Titi had told me about her dilemma. I was so sad for her. When I got there she was a mess. Her normally pristine apartment was in a state of chaos and even her fridge was completely empty. She actually looked like she had lost quite a bit of weight.

Amaka wasn't surprised that I knew what was going on. I explained that I just wanted her to know that I was there for her if she needed me. After we spoke, I made her go and lie down while I cleaned up her place and cooked some pepper soup. Amaka couldn't believe it all when she re-emerged, looking fresher and more relaxed. She couldn't believe that I had come to visit her, much less cleaned up. It was funny when she looked at me strangely and said, "Something is different about you."

And that is when it fell out of my mouth: "I am different. I have realized that I am blessed."

Titi

A new start

I got my commission check this morning. Let me tell you I had to rejoice. Because Dele and his Mrs. chose so many upgrades, my check was even larger than I thought it would be. As I recalled the whole thing with Dele, I smiled. My stupidity had not been for nothing; at least I had the good sense to sell the man a mansion!

The check came at the right time because I really needed some good news after everything I had gone through with Segun. Unfortunately I couldn't really celebrate. I had to go and meet Amaka down at the Planned Parenthood Clinic.

I can so understand her decision. It is hard to raise a child on your own. I know it wasn't easy for Amaka to decide this, so I don't expect anyone to judge her. Surprisingly, even Mina has been completely supportive. She says she doesn't agree with the decision but recognizes that the choice is not hers to make, and that she would be in Amaka's corner no matter what.

We sat in the waiting area of the clinic as we waited for Amaka's name to be called. There were so many people also waiting: an African couple, two teenage girls smacking their gum loudly and talking about having an abortion like it was as simple as going to the grocery store. They had obviously done it multiple times because they were trying to trump each other with stories about their procedures.

I was appalled. Amaka was nervously thumbing through a magazine but I knew she could hear them as they described the experience in graphic detail. Just when I was about to go up and complain to the nurse, they called Amaka's name. She had to go into the room alone. She walked slowly and heavily towards the door leading to the inner sanctum of the clinic, and I watched her sadly.

A year later

Titi

And so it went

So much has happened, where do I start? First off, I actually started my own real estate firm. I am so psyched!

I got a big contract with a national builder to represent them in a multi-phase project. I mean, we are talking about close to 500 homes! Did I say God is so good!!! Yes O, I have become a churchgoer. I may not be saved and sanctified, but I know God is real.

You'll never guess what else? Remember Emmanuel, the maintenance man in my building? After everything that happened with Dele and Segun, I decided to forget about my rich man criteria. So I said yes when he asked me out and we've been going strong for quite a few months now.

He is truly the most amazing man I have ever known. We have these deep conversations and he is so sweet to me. Okay, here is the main gist, don't fall down when I tell you O…we have not had sex yet. We both decided that we would abstain. I won't lie O, it has been really hard but honestly it's like I am seeing a whole new side of myself. I finally understand that I have so much to offer besides my body.

There is more gist O, yes, my people, I have been saving the best for last. Emmanuel, the maintenance man, was really a doctor from Nigeria taking his USMLE exams. Can you believe it! He didn't tell me until recently because he wanted to make sure he passed them first. You see, all that searching and what I was looking for was right here underneath my nose.

As for Mina; where do I start? She and Obinna are still sorting themselves out, she has been a little closed-lipped on their divorce proceedings but Carolina has since had the baby, a boy.

But while things may still be up in the air for Mina, she is far from devastated. She's been certified in Interior Décor, since she had such a knack for it already and you know what -- I introduced her to my builder and they contracted with her to furnish all their model homes! My girl is totally on her way. I am so happy for her. What's more, you wouldn't even recognize her today if you saw her. She wears her hair loose and flowing now, smiles all the time and I do believe that she has even put on a few pounds. I guess she has finally begun to relax.

That leaves me with my dear Maksy. Well, she is the reason I am putting on my best church suit and hat-- and

I must say I am working this Nanette Lepore yellow tweed suit. It's quirky but it is so flattering to my figure. Emmanuel will be here any minute and I hope he is wearing the yellow tie I gave him. It is very important that we look good. After all, it is not every day that I get to be the Godmother of a beautiful baby girl.

Amaka named her Ginikanwa, which means in Igbo, 'what is better than a child.'

As for me, you know, always keeping it funky, I call her Gigi!

Mina

Joy comes in the morning

I have to tell you that my life has completely changed. I have been going to church and it's helping me become centered somehow. I even spoke to my mother after many months and even though she was still quite nasty, I have found a way to forgive her. She got really quiet when I told her, so maybe there's still hope for us. Since then we've fallen into a bit of a routine. I call her every Sunday after church and we talk for a bit. We never mention money or Uncle Tosan. Instead I tell her about the sermon and my new business.

Speaking of new business, I love decorating other people's houses. Titi got me a big contract doing model homes for her builder and recently I have gotten a couple of clients on my own. Last month I actually netted four thousand dollars. I couldn't believe it. Of course I've had to scale down. I can no longer afford my previous home, but my Dunwoody condo is lovely and when I come home I feel more secure in its coziness than I ever did before.

Obinna came to visit yesterday. No, we aren't divorced yet. Actually I don't know what we are doing right now. Ever since I apologized to him, it's like we are starting afresh. I see him with new eyes. He is so kind and decent, and really quite wonderful. I don't know how I missed all this before. I think he is seeing me with new eyes too, because something totally unexpected has happened -- sparks have started to fly between us.

Yesterday, he came over and I happened to be making dinner, so I asked him if he wanted to join me and as he sat down to a meal of jollof rice and fried goat meat, he suddenly reached over and held my hands. I was so surprised I just looked at him wondering what was going on. He looked at me like he had on our wedding day and I started feeling like I should have felt on that same day.

I felt like a silk cloth was slowly being pulled over my body. The feeling was sweet yet a little painful. I started to pull my hand away. I wasn't expecting to feel like that towards Obinna; after all he had never interested me in the past, but he held on tight.

"Mina," he said, looking at me in a manner that was unsure yet determined. "I've been thinking," he said, pausing to take a deep breath. Then he said, "I love you and I would like for us to try again. You don't have to answer right now, but I have been thinking about this for a long time."

I couldn't believe my ears. "What are you saying?" I asked, not really sure of what response I wanted to hear.

The truth was I had realized that I had fallen in love with my husband, after he had moved in with another woman and had a baby. I was loath to admit it because it was so crazy -- who falls in love with their spouse after they have left? He was looking at me as if waiting for an answer. I just stared at him, that sweet smile, strong arms. He was still my husband but was I ready to go back into a relationship with him, especially with him having a baby outside our marriage? Would it not be better to start fresh with someone else?

"Will the Godparents please rise?" The Reverend's request jolted me back to reality. Titi and I stood up. I looked up at Amaka, standing there all alone, holding her daughter. She looked resplendent in her emerald green chiffon boubou. Her mother had brought it as a gift when she came to help her with the child.

She looked over at us and I gave her a big smile. I was so proud of her. It had been a difficult year for her but she had done it. In the hospital, after the baby had just been born and when Amaka was still woozy from the drugs and the delivery, she said to me: "I know what people will say about my baby and me, but Mina, everything I did, I did out of love."

Amaka

Worthwhile

It was all worth it. As I hold my darling daughter in my hands, that's all I can think -- it was all worth it. All the tears I have shed this past year. All the yelling, screaming and even the drama! And believe me there was a lot of drama: from Jeffrey's wife threatening me on the phone, to my mother refusing to talk to me for months because of the shame she felt I had brought on the family.

It was a horrible year. I can't believe I am here, carrying my baby. We made it! I am so glad I walked out of the clinic when I did. I am not judging anyone who felt like they had to follow through with that choice; but for me, it wasn't right. I was acting out of fear and thank God, He gave me the courage to go forward with the pregnancy.

I can't lie; it was the hardest thing I have had to do in my life. Just telling my mom alone was heart wrenching.

I was so ashamed at work, having a child with no husband. For a while I couldn't hold my head up.

During labor when other women had their husbands rubbing their backs, I had no man; but fortunately I had two women, my girls, Mina and Titi. They got me through and they are still getting me through. That's why I made them the Godparents. My daughter may not have a father, but she has three mothers and hopefully that will make up for things.

It has been a hard road and my load is still heavy but in spite of everything I feel light. Not just because of my baby, though she is a wondrous blessing to me. I feel light also because the weight of expectations has been lifted. I have done the worst thing possible. I have broken virtually every norm about what *good girls* do. It's almost like now I can begin to live. I have finally dictated life on my own terms. Of course, this is not the path I would have taken but I guess it was the path that was necessary.

Jeffrey is completely out of our life and I like it like that. I know people look at me and gossip about me in my unwed state, but I don't care. I don't care what my mother thinks or anyone else for that matter. It has taken a lot for me to come to this place where I am finally comfortable with my life. One thing Jeffrey did do was send a substantial check for "the child" as he put it in the letter.

He was basically washing his hands of me and trying to redeem himself at the same time. I felt like taking the check and ripping it up, but I beg, I be Naija girl. Money na money! So I took a leave of absence after the baby was born to take courses at the famed Atlanta Culinary Institute. I may not have the man of my dreams yet, but I can still pursue my other dreams.

My life is good and I am thankful. Every time I look into my Gigi's gurgling, cooing face, my little edible adorable darling, I know what real love feels like.

Life is funny, isn't it? It took me getting in the ugliest of situations for me to realize that marriage is one thing, but it is love that really matters.